# BLACK WIDOW'S GHOST

I0770921

BY

*J.K. RENNAKER*

Copyright © 2025 J.K. Rennaker

All rights reserved.

ISBN: 978-1-967632-25-1

Printed in the United States of America. No part of this publication shall be reproduced, transmitted, or sold in whole or in part in any form without the prior written consent of the author, except as provided by the United States of America copyright law. Any unauthorized usage of the text without express written permission of the publisher is a violation of the author's copyright and is illegal and punishable by law. All trademarks and registered trademarks appearing in this guide are the property of their respective owners.

# Table of Contents

# Author's Note

Black Widow's Ghost is a work of fiction. The condition referred to as Cognitive Dissociative Disorder is entirely fictional. The intention in creating a fictional term was to address the unique narrative of the book, its main characters, and those who interact with them in a non-triggering way. It is not a depiction of Dissociative Identity Disorder (DID) or any other real-life mental health condition. It does not address the issue of mental health or any treatments for mental health. This fictional diagnosis allows space to explore themes of identity, control, and trauma without making assumptions about or misrepresenting real-world experiences. If you or someone you know is living with a Dissociative Disorder, you deserve empathy, understanding, and care. I would also like to acknowledge the presence of a transgender character in a central and complex role. While one of their identities plays a part in one of the story's darker elements, it is never my intent to suggest that trans identity itself is a source of danger or villainy. Trans people, like all people, deserve representation that reflects their full humanity, encompassing strength, love, vulnerability, and complexity. The character develops their identity through experiences of manipulation, trauma, and survival, not by their gender identity. The transgender character is shaped by her own experiences as a human being, much like the experiences I have had in my own life as a non-binary person of color in a small rural town. The story explores issues with identity, agency, and psychological control in heightened fictional terms. If you are navigating this world as a trans person, you deserve love, dignity, and support —something I deeply value as a storyteller.

Thank you for reading.

*J.K. Rennaker*

# Chapter One-The Garden of Eden

The seeming normality of something by day can give way to the carnality of night. By sunrise or sunset, the top of a typical rock can have the benign appearance of granite, quartz, or something altogether different. It looks harmless and unobtrusive, yet once a need to change the angle of vision arises, when it gets in the way of said progress, and piques the interest of a passerby, the dark, dirty underside begins to reveal itself. The dark side teems with life. Until that one curious person or animal bumps it, picks it up, turns it over, or moves it, the underside of the rock remains relatively unnoticed. Underneath lies some of the most fascinating and dangerous creatures of the dirt. Slugs, earwigs, earthworms, microorganisms, strugglers, smugglers, and predators, all hurrying and scurrying to escape their fate, moving to stay out of the light for fear of exposure or death.

Do not judge the appearance of seemingly lifeless rock. What is underneath can be seen. First, the angle of vision must change. Curiosity turns it over and looks beyond the surface. The Lido is one such rock. What is a Lido? Well, on the surface, it is quiet. It seems like a sleepy little alleyway with only a set of steel double Doors. It is topped by a velvet awning featuring an elaborate "L" in embroidery on the front side. People are walking by it without notice. The busy streets and honking automobiles are moving in both directions, unaware of driving past the entrance of one of the swankiest nightclubs in Chicago. It escapes their attention because it rests at the end of an alley amid the trash bins and crates. It does not boast of unique architecture or a prestigious location. Harsh reality likes to eat out of its bins and sleep under its fire escapes.

Steam from the depths of the city's irritable bowels creeps up through the grates, creating a backdrop for a sinister scene. Yes, during the day the Lido is just an address in a zone, in an insignificant part of "Chi Town"—just a half a block from "the surface of the rock"—the bright, warm, safe, surface of high-rise apartments and office buildings. People are hurrying and scurrying to fulfill their destinies—perhaps make a buck or two. They want to make it to the end of their shift—the stuff between coffee breaks and needing to be done before the next cigarette break. Then, they feel it. Somehow, they know. The rock is turning. Life choices made will become manifested. Promises and deals are made and broken.

Within hours, the damage begins to take its toll. The reality is that there is risk involved. Unpredictable outcomes are certain. They prepare for it. They welcome it and loathe it simultaneously. The sun fades and begins to fall past the horizon. Locks and latches on closets get unlocked. People dress up and call their transport. The children of the night emerge from the shadows, protected by the half-light. It is all about the hunt—looking for John, looking for a morsel, looking for a bed, finding a trap! Others only come to visit the underside of the rock. They bring their insatiable curiosity and their penchant for excitement to avoid the soiling of their reputations. They make up stories to tell their spouses, parents, and themselves about why they must venture out and find that new and exciting thing—hoisting up sails and letting the wind take them where destiny awaits. They are making up lies to tell, because no one knows what mysteries the nighttime holds for those who dare to turn over the rock. For some, it is an undeniable curiosity. For others, it is an addiction that needs a fix.

The staff remove the garbage and clean up the alley. Two gentlemen roll out the red carpet for the VIP guests, and after a while, what appears to be a sleepy little alley transforms into one of the trendiest night spots in the heart of the Windy City. The rock continues to turn, and the neon lights illuminate the darkness, revealing the life of the creatures of the night as they converge in a single space.

The Lido is a palace of glamour and seduction. Club Bunnies hop from rock to rock to satisfy their animal taste and lust after their insatiable desires, with predators waiting in the shadows. The valets are parking the vehicles with open palms—cash tips and stock tips. There are earthworms, slugs, drugs, crickets, sex, dirt, mud, mugs of sorrow sliding down tender throats. Excitement and release beckon, but the night is young and the city is still waking up. The hedons have chosen rain to fall on the night crawlers to enhance the stench. All will miss the presence of stars tonight. Even in night's sleepiness, life is rife and ready to be tested. Some fears must be faced. Depending on the viewer's angle, some struggles end up as wins rather than losses.

The night, unlike the goal-seeking, denial-hungry citizens of the top of the rock, is a game of survival fueled by drugs and adrenaline. The city is unforgiving and not safe for the children of the streets. It can be as cold as the Chicago rain that chooses to fall on this night. The rain falls on the makeup of the scurriers and patrons' glistening leather and rubber costumes. They are rushing to save their soaked images. Their pace is quickening with the faster-falling rain. If they cannot navigate the turning of the rock, the rock will destroy them. Once they fall, the merciless squashing begins, people lose their path, or a foul or fiend may devour them. Ironically, "Dayers" get accreditation for having more intelligence than their darker dwelling counterparts. However, "Nighters" have their capacity for gut instinct and intense desire to survive. It has given them a specific intelligence that should not, by any means, be ruled out or discounted.

The Lido is solid ground—a lighthouse for those who only come out at night. For a price, it is a haven for those who need shelter from the dark side of the rock. It is the bustling center of nightlife and "night-lifers." It is a visual beacon to the weary, wet walkers, "Dayers" masquerading as "Nighters." The appeal, most definitely, is the fact that there is such a wide array of lust seekers and sexual adventurers. They gather to celebrate the night-- and more arrive by the hour. Victims are seen rubbing shoulders with the predators. The Hunters are mingling with the hunted, and the voyeurs—just an arm's length away from the exhibitionists. It is a writhing and heaving nest of vipers, all of them under the spell of The Lido's sexual atmosphere. Is it a sex club? A scene for sinners? Absolutely! It is the perfect place to meet the rare and precious insect! There are no lines to cross. There are no boundaries here. The only way to get through it unharmed is to surrender to the good time. Check in the overcoat, Release inhibition, and leave expectation and judgment at the door. For here, nothing is what it appears to be, and being unprepared will shake the foundations of knowledge to the very core. Once the rock turns, it reveals the dirty underworld of the night crawlers. There is little one can do but hold on to sanity for dear life. Pray that sanity remains when the rock goes back from whence it came. And then the rain stops.

Once the darkness takes over, "the life" dominates all who venture into it. After enjoying a few moments in full cadence, the real beauties of the night take center stage.

Halfway into the half-light, the illusionists start weaving their webs of seduction. They hope to lure a willing visitor or trap a prize stallion. With their eyes heavily painted and their gestures hypnotic, they perform the siren songs of yesterday for all of the passing sailors in town. The ritualistic traditions they cling to make them the shamans of the nightlife. Here is where a lost adventurer can find their way back home. However, it comes with a price. These "would-be women" are poetry in motion—with a vengeance. They are the Hollywood glamour dolls—the supermodel vixens of the street. They capture the attention of many a soul that dares to peer into their "house of cards". They are precious stones. They are shiny and sought after. They are alluring and engaging. However, there is also a grimy side, as deep and dark as hell itself.

Now and then, these rare and beautiful insects attach to a political figure or sports celebrity, draining the life from their host. To think they are hideous morphs, as the tabloids portray, is to underestimate them. If they are as the stereotype suggests, their efforts remain without reward, and we can ignore it and all go about our business. Not the case—clearly. They have all of the equipment to get where they need to be. They take their place in the grand scheme of things along with detectives, hit men, and even college sweethearts and white supremacists. Fragile and hanging in the balance, the casual observer decides that they have seen enough of the underside of the rock. They think they can return it to its rightful place, and nothing will be disturbed—putting it back will not harm whatever is scurrying underneath. This naive self-centeredness contributes to separating the sunny side of the stone from the dark side.

Every stone has a dark side. Detectives use the phrase "leave no stone unturned." Their jobs are to solve mysteries. A good detective is not afraid to explore both sides of the rock to get to the truth. It is a special instinct that allows them to connect to the seedy world of the night. They have access without actually disturbing the stone. People marvel at their uncanny ability to gather clues and solve crimes given merely a "trail of breadcrumbs" and hunches. It seems they have endless energy and resources—things they must leave behind at the end of the day. They go home to their wives and children, enjoying the separation of 'nightlife' and 'daytime surface' dwelling. Nevertheless, their experiences come with a price as well. Aside from the customary health issues, there is the emotional toll. They immerse themselves in cultures that do not appeal to them to gather the information they need to complete a case; their job forces them to see—and sometimes do—things that most people avoid. The "dayers" pass judgment on the "night-lifers" in their ongoing battle for the soul of the sinner. Detectives, however, remain objective, even passive. It is all in the name of truth and justice.

Detective Dwight Husselman is well aware of the dangers inherent in his chosen line of work. He cannot see as well as he used to. He has flashbacks and past experiences haunting him constantly. He suffers from night terrors. His night terrors are real and taken from the pages of his life. Until this night, he can pacify his dark subconscious as part of the job. Usually, the night sweats pass with the completion of each case. This night is different. Rain triggers this one. The rain brings the third installment of a series of nightmares. The second one happened only last night. There are waves of shooting pain starting from his hip. As his dark visions dance around in his mind, the pain gradually becomes more intense. Dwight's brow seizes. He grits his teeth. His breathing is heavy now. His heartbeat is increasing in tempo. Enhanced by the thunder, rising with every toss and turn, Dwight can feel the blood rushing to his face and other parts of his anatomy.

He twists the sheets until the defenses of the body and mind begin to take over. Without warning, he sits up in bed and yells out with his masculine voice: "Cassy, No!" Two words joining in sheer terror—unlocking themselves and escaping—after years of repression.

There is now a bittersweet emotion electrifying the air. He fools himself into thinking the lightning is the catalyst behind his outburst. The flashes greet his face and illuminate his wife's horrified, frozen expression. A pale moonlight from the street outside their flat in Chicago shines on his wife, Misty's face. She stares at him, waiting for his explanation. Her eyes are following him. For Dwight, this is a new pattern of behavior that she must now categorize and file under "disturbing behavior."

Dwight tries to scramble for something to say that relieves the awkwardness permeating the atmosphere of the room and the surprise between his legs. He tries, but he cannot hide what is protruding from between his manly thighs. He was erect. However, his dismay turned to salvation. There is a buildup of fluid in his bladder. He has to bolt for the bathroom or he will soak his sheets and his wife. He immediately breaks for his "porcelain buddy" and closes the door—he sighs of relief that he is saving his wife from further embarrassment. Misty was only slightly stunned. The vision of feminine beauty, with auburn hair and piercing green eyes, sits in astonishment as she watches her mature, well-adjusted detective husband bolt out of the room, much like a schoolgirl bolting out of gym class, because her "friend Flo" has decided to drop in for an unexpected visit. Misty smiles cheekily, realizes what Dwight said during his nightmare, and returns her gaze to her husband. "Who did he say?" Misty asked herself.

She ponders the implications of the name "Cassy" or any other words that do not directly pertain to her. She thought that maybe Dwight was reliving a past case—if he knew what was good for him. After giving it a little thought, she realizes this is probably related to Dwight's nightmares the past few nights. The choice is hers. One, decide if she is curious enough to pick up this rock and turn it over. Two, leave the stone in its place, undisturbed.

If Misty chooses option one, she might subject herself to the irreversible effects of the grime found on the underbelly of the rock. She will also expose herself to the idea of this mysterious "Cassy" creature. She is curious if this "Cassy" is "venomous" and causes harm to her children, her husband, or herself. She knows that the stone's position is forever changed once it is picked up, and it cannot return to the same way. One stone turns. Then, another stone accidentally gets moved, and another, and so on. Suddenly, the foundation on which families have arduously built their existence is in total upheaval. There is no solid ground anymore. It becomes a psychotic freefall of the mind, and anarchy of the heart.

Misty stares into the room's darkness at the rectangular halo of light around their bathroom door. She tries to scramble up something to say that will sound invitingly neutral and somewhat objective. Dwight is going through something very serious at work or personally, but, knowing Dwight, it is probably a small amount of both. Dwight takes his work very seriously but never brings it home or to bed with him. In the past, Dwight told her stories of times when he went through periods of self-discovery. On the surface, he comes back unharmed. Later on, he meets Misty and the two settle down together to have a normal life for all intents and purposes. Their friends and family often comment on how Dwight and Misty's relationship seems "solid as a rock." Misty is so happy that she has finally found the man of her dreams. Dwight is satisfied that he has found someone not soiled by the cold, grimy, and tarnished life this world can dish out.

Our detective is strong, intelligent, and invincible. He is a relatively new and eager detective. He knew that when he was recently appointed to the Chicago Police force, he would get to see firsthand what people only see on "Cop Shows" and in true crime novels. He will be responsible for "saving the world" and leaving no stone unturned. There is no way to estimate the collateral damage these cases cause, both emotionally and physically. This night is no exception. Hearing moans from the bathroom asking for aspirin, Misty sighs in relief that she at least knows the answer to that question. The other questions continue to elude her.

"In the cabinet!" She says in a voice loud enough to carry but soft enough not to wake the children. As to inquiring about his well-being, Misty just asked him the generally objective yet painfully vague question. "Are you okay?"

"I am fine," Dwight answers predictably. Misty's dissatisfaction with Dwight's answer is evident in her responseless silence. Conversational chess is not her forte. Dwight, however, was a master. He learned this skill during many years as a beat cop before becoming a detective. Building a career from the ground up requires the life skill of reading between the lines—instincts that remain to this day unmatched and, ultimately, led to his promotion to detective.

Misty's instincts are very feminine. They come from that familial place in the abdomen, and they serve her well. Over the years, especially as a detective's wife and mother of two children, she has honed her skills to a fine point, which leads her to capture the heart of Chicago's finest hero.

"Another nightmare? You know you have been having these episodes more frequently. Is it something we can talk about? Are things okay at.. " Dwight interrupts her plea for open communication.

"No, Honey. Everything is fine."

The truth is, Dwight knows that Misty does not want to know the answer to the question that she asks. She is an amazing wife, so she coaxes, wanting to share her husband's burdens, while bracing herself for the unexpected and possibly bizarre response. In his line of work, there is no telling. Dwight would not know what to say to her. He does not know what the nightmares mean. He shoves two white pills down his throat, hoping that they are sleeping pills. He looks in the mirror and asks himself, "Am I losing it?"

There are many nights that Dwight stares at the ceiling, contemplating the thought of seeing a (he hates to even say the word) therapist. Agreeing to meet with a psychoanalyst is admitting to Dwight that he has failed in life—he is defeated and is giving up. The dark side is hindering his ability to cope with the stress of the job. It is a policeman's way of saying, "You are weak and less of a man."

Although he knows that his friends and family will offer their support, he will not jeopardize his heroic image and possibly raise doubts among the police commissioner and his peers. He cannot bear the idea of "the guys" giving him "sideways glances"-wondering if he can "cut the mustard." Yes, his pride continues to keep him from it. The pain still pulses from his hips. His epiphany is reflected on his face as a triumphant expression. Dwight discovers that the cause of his excruciating pain is the piercing of one of nature's eight-legged beasts, a spider. His foe must have been hiding under the sheets.

Dwight's nightmare, the tossing and turning, must have aggravated the brown recluse. This bombardment only contributes to the events of the night. He captures the enemy and places it in a glass mason jar, a prison cell for spiders. He twists the lid, closes it tight, and gets dressed. Misty looks on in angst for a definitive clue. She waits. Dwight comes out of the bathroom, cursing and shaking his shirt. He puts it on cautiously. His pants are on, and he is belting his shirt inside the pants. Misty assumes he is not going to work. He walks over and sits next to Misty on the bed. Each sock goes on with sharp jolts of pain. A few red bumps are starting to form on his hip. Misty hears him ranting under his breath and knows it has something to do with the nightmare. He is going somewhere. He leaves in the middle of the night sometimes. This time, he hurries with greater speed and urgency. Goose pimples begin to rise on her skin.

"Honey, have you seen our insurance cards?"

"Top desk drawer."

"I got bit by a spider. Need to get it checked out."

"Black Widow? Was it a Black Widow?"

"Nah. worse. a brown recluse."

"Do you want me to go with you?"

"No, no. Don't get up, sweetheart. I can get there."

"Well, take your phone and keep me posted. You can call me and let me know that you are okay. Can you do that for me, please?"

"Sure thing."

He leans in to kiss Misty goodbye. Another shooting pain hits him in the thigh again. He winces. She kisses him anyway. Misty answers the questions like a game show contestant. The prize, however, offers no reward. When Dwight talks of the bite on his thigh, he has proof that it is indeed a brown recluse. Misty speaks of the bite from the nightmare. It seems more like a black widow, and she would also be exactly right. Dwight puts on his overcoat. The phone rings, and Misty rushes for it before it wakes the children. They are probably aware of the movement in their townhouse at 4 a.m., just in case, she dives for the call and picks up the receiver. Only calls from the precinct come through at this hour, when there is breaking news of a fresh case or some emergency.

Dwight finishes rearranging the sleeves on his jacket. He shakes the bulk of the woolen exterior onto his broad chest and linebacker shoulders. He makes his way past the bedroom and stops in his tracks. Misty tells the caller to wait a minute. Dwight was unable to make it out of the doorway. He froze as he approached the threshold from the bedroom to the hallway just outside. Misty pulls the phone away from her ear and looks at Dwight with his hand on the door. Standing in the hallway's light just outside, Misty hands him the phone. She watches him. It amazes her how calm he remains when facing a phone call like this. The information that one of these calls can render is enough to give dry heaves to a normal individual of good constitution. Dwight remains calm and cool. Details of a new case, relayed over the conversation, changed his expression from objectivity to disbelief. He is now a child picking up a rock. He turns it over only to find dirt, grime, and every kind of disgusting creature crawling around. Slugs, spiders, worms, silverfish, and centipedes are too many to mention and to name. Dwight's detective side fascinates Misty the most. The macabre that surfaces in him makes him mysterious and extremely sexy, from the approach to the phone to the muffled sound of the caller's voice on the other end, changing his expression. She was smitten.

The gist of the conversation is that two dock workers on the north side of town were loading some pallets onto a barge when one of them spots a dark object at the end of a pier. It is raining, and from a distance, the two workers cannot clearly see the object in detail. So, they approach the object. As the workers approach, they realize it is the body of a woman. They immediately called the police. The police arrive within minutes. They quarantine the area, and the person at the end of the phone call requests Dwight's presence at the scene. The background noise sounds like mayhem. Misty studies Dwight's expression as he ends the call and approaches her. He looks calm and warm. He is sensitive to her expressions. He is the Dwight she fell in love with. He gives her a look. He does not say much. She returns his gaze and says that she understands that he must go. She says she loves him and reminds him to get his bite checked before it becomes a problem. Dwight complies. He sneaks another kiss before turning away. He walks down the hall to the street. Misty whispers a prayer under her breath to bring her husband home unharmed.

The rain stops. He arrives, greeted by several policemen who escort him to the crime scene. The victim has long, dark hair. It is matted and tangled from the rain. Dwight talks to one of the officers. The dark coat has money in one of the pockets. The other pocket has a diamond ring. The coroner's van arrives and takes the body to the morgue at Mercy Medical Center. There is no documentation to identify the body of the victim. The only witnesses were the two dock workers. For all they knew, it could have been a suicide. The policeman entered the statements of the two dock workers into the record. Daylight begins to ascend upon the city. Dwight grabs a cup of coffee and heads toward headquarters. Jerry Mack and the "team" wait patiently for the details gathered to be revealed, anxious for the investigation to get underway.

# Chapter Two-What We Know

Police commissioners, like other professionals, are complex individuals at best and are often misunderstood. One has to be focused yet observant, commanding yet approachable, detached yet humane. It's a high-wire act to be sure. The balancing pole is one's ability to "know" the people you work with. Instincts will dictate your actions when reasoning and senses fail you. Gerald McCafferney (or "Jerry Mack") attributes a large part of his recent promotion to Police Commissioner to his ability to "get a read" on people. He can size a person up in five seconds or less. He can tell when he is being lied to or when someone withholds facts that could be vital to a case. This skill, which he has mastered, is one that he hopes to pass on to the young people who will, one day, be his replacements when he retires.

However, Jerry Mack's finely-honed instincts don't come without a price. Aside from the routine insomnia and night sweats, he suffers from high blood pressure and occasional erectile dysfunction, for which he is currently taking medication. Yep, the years have taken their toll on him, but he knows that, in life, this was his calling. Jerry Mack is not only the new Chicago Police Commissioner but also a hunter. He recalls the early days of being a newly appointed detective, when he hunted serial killers and rapists—praying on the innocent citizens of Chicago and the surrounding neighborhoods and suburbs. He chased thieves like prize bucks, keeping a special drawer in the filing cabinet marked "Trophy Room". He occasionally opened it up and reviewed the files with a sense of nostalgia. The more arrogant the perpetrator, the more bizarre the modus operandi, the more memorable the experience, and the "sweeter the victory," the greater the "Spoils."

He saw his early detective days in the eyes of everyone in that room. He pondered the experiences that await these young people, some barely out of college. He felt the apprehension on their behalf, foreseeing the events that would shape their careers and sharpen their skills; unwelcome, but necessary. The things they must endure will forever alter their perception of their fellow man. They will experience the brutality that man can inflict on one another. They will see the underside of the rock and never be fully prepared for what they will encounter. He wonders: Out of everyone in that room, looking through the Venetian blinds and glass window of his office—who will have the stamina to make it as far as he did— Police Commissioner."We will see...Dammit! We will see," he said under his breath.

He looked around the room and held a Styrofoam cup of coffee with creamer to his lips. After taking a sip, he burned his lip and cursed so loudly that everyone in the briefing room could hear him. They turned to look, and Jerry looked back in embarrassment. Now is as good a time as any to start the meeting. In the early days, he hunted alone or with a partner. The best thing about his new position was that he could now hunt in packs. The work would be easier for him. He had teams of detectives, criminologists, pathologists, sketch artists, and problem-solving civilians waiting to help. There were plain-clothed and uniformed officers, S.W.A.T. Units, D.E.A. operatives, K-9 Units, undercover officers, you name it. Most importantly, he had The Law on his side. Now he could "bring down the big game," and the damage to himself, emotionally and physically, would be considerably reduced.

This team represented his eyes, legs, and arms, with these parts now more reliable than his own. Yes, no matter what, serving justice was essential to him. He didn't see himself doing anything else. Like everyone here, he felt it was his God-given duty to make the world—Chicago, at least—a less fearful place, like his family for three generations. It has taken him quite a few years to amass this team of young detectives, all of whom he saw in that conference room this morning. In less than an instant, he could see their faces and recall some of the landmark cases that he worked on with them, individually and in the typical teams of two. These "kids" were bound by their desire for justice. Additionally, the pride that comes from them demonstrates that they are willing to be led by their "Chieftain" and bring another evil criminal to justice.

The respectful hush of anticipation filled the air as they awaited the details of the next top priority case. All races and personality types were represented in the group, waiting for the first order of business. Jerry wanted to hug them all and tell them how proud he was to be in the company of some of the sharpest minds in law enforcement. However, his face remained expressionless out of respect for the victim they will meet today. He made his way to the podium at the other end of a room that resembled a high school classroom from the 1960s. There was a long table running down the center of the room, with several chairs on both sides and an overhead projector at one end, facing a five-foot projection screen. Everyone focused all their attention forward as Jerry Mack turned on the overhead projector and showed the first slide of the victim. The lights dimmed.

"What you are looking at, Gentlemen, and Ladies, is the body of one Jimmy Rantor. A street punk, he lived in a one-bedroom apartment over 14th Street. Before that, he was on the streets, living in alleys and sleeping under fire escapes. He lurks in and around a nightclub called "The Lido." He is a twenty-two-year-old Caucasian male. He was found at the tip of Pier #14 at 6 AM this morning by a fisherman who began the day late because of inclement weather. They found him wearing heavy makeup streaming down his face, causing lines and smearing. The significance is that this happened before the rain started."

Dwight didn't know if it was the words "makeup" or "Lido" that triggered his anxiety, but the expression on his face had turned from objective disinterest to guilty concealment. The words of the Commissioner seemed to fade in the distance, becoming muted and unintelligible. His stomach began to twist and heave like cramps after a rigorous workout. He could feel his temperature rising higher and higher. He felt that everyone could read his thoughts, and at any minute, they would turn around and stare at him in disgust. Should he fabricate an excuse and try to exit the meeting? Or should he try to "Stick it out" and hope that his culpable body language will not choose to betray him, like a child stealing cookies and getting caught?

The Commissioner continued. "Jimmy started as a drifter with no real friends or family to speak of—no one came to claim the body. Typically, we lack the time and resources to conduct a thorough investigation in cases like this one. However, we will list it in the press and gather information as it becomes available. We will follow up on leads and gather background information to try to determine a person of interest, most likely a fellow street hustler with whom he may have had an altercation, which resulted in his death. Maybe he owed this P.O.I. (person of interest) money and couldn't pay up."

"Yeah, but...Why the heavy makeup?"

"We aren't sure at this time. Could be a "calling card." Hopefully, someone will come forward who has the information we need to enlighten us."

Dwight was having trouble focusing on the debriefing. He kept drifting in thoughts to a case in his past that would change his life and his view of the world forever. It became one of the reasons our detective had become the tough, hard-edged, hard-nosed investigator he is now. He was just finishing up a high-profile serial rapist/ murderer case long before he met his wife, Misty.

He had difficulty identifying the perpetrator and where he would strike next. The rapist had not established a pattern of any kind. The attacks happened at random times. He chose women of all backgrounds and levels of society. He was elusive, intelligent, arrogant, and perhaps Dwight's biggest challenge. The rapist, Trevor Whitney, went to great lengths to plan his attacks. Always staying one step ahead of Dwight and his expert team of investigators, he planned every detail of his assaults thoroughly. He executed them with precision and meticulous attention to detail. Physically, he was surprisingly average-looking. Seemingly, the most docile of all of Earth's creatures. However, his victims were savagely tortured and beaten within an inch of their lives. They were toyed with and then snuffed out. All except one.

Dwight could add this Trophy to his collection because of this one survivor—perhaps his most excellent capture to date. It also garnered the admiration of his peers and the adulation of the Chicago Metro Police Force. As the briefing continued, Dwight journeyed in his mind to a place that had remained undisturbed for so long, and which had now been opened up once again by the trigger words in Jerry Mack's presentation. It had been buried so deep in his memory that the only way to free those mental prisoners of social oppression—in Dwight's mental place where all repressed memories go—is for God, conscience, or Karma or whatever force guides the universe, to find the key and let them loose to be acknowledged and reconciled at last—the place where the "Lone Survivor" was filed away in his memory banks as a moment of "self-discovery."

Dwight allowed his feelings for the victim to interfere with the objectivity of a budding, yet ambitious, young detective. He was like a boy taking his first piano lesson in her presence. However, he had the body of a college wide receiver—at least that is what the victim told Dwight face to face. Dwight recalled that her eyes seemed to smile when she made this revelation to him. She couldn't have stood more than five feet six inches tall in high heels.

A delicate wisp of down from a young hatchling slowly muddied and crushed under the weight of the rock, underneath which she lived. To think of her made his heart quiver. Memories of her made his body whine for the attention she gave him. She left no part of him untouched—even now. It was the mist after the rain. A cold, droll mist that chilled one to the bone. Dwight had been feverishly piecing together clues from the Trevor Whitney rapes, but he knew that without a positive I.D. there was no way to convict him. All of the evidence they had was circumstantial. No one had seen him or witnessed any of the incidents.

Dwight had hit a brick wall in his investigation, and none of the clues he had were able to reveal to him Trevor Whitney's next move. Frustrated, tired, and hungry, Dwight had started packing his notes and things for the night and headed for the door, determining that there was no more he could do now. That was until the phone rang again. It seemed that the thirteenth precinct had picked up a "911" call from a rape victim whose description fit the modus operandi of Trevor Whitney. However, the victim, in this case, survived the assault, managed to escape, and called for help. Dwight prepared himself to meet with this sole survivor and shed some light on her assailant and why she was able to escape. Expectations were high. Her eyewitness account was essential to the case, but Dwight had to convince her to testify against him in court to get a conviction. As excited as Dwight was to finally have an end to this case, putting another predator away, he was also curious about why she had been "let go." Why did he not take her life as he did the others? He was a cold and heartless manipulator of people and clues. Why her? Why would a predator with this level of intelligence choose to let one of his victims go (according to her statement)? It was no accident.

Sometimes weeks before the actual assault, rape, torture and eventual slaying, he stalked them. There must have been something about this victim that was different enough to make him change his mind and let her go.

Dwight wasted no time getting to the station across town. The paparazzi had gotten wind of the story and had already arrived at the station and started setting up on the steps of the building, in the cold, misty dawn—the media frenzy of the year. All of the networks were anxious to get the scoop on this single, mysterious female survivor and how she became the one that got away. Dwight managed to push through the crowd and enter the police station. The popularity of this case had the precinct in an uproar. Clerks were hosting the hordes of relentless media while also trying to do their regular jobs. Security had begun to move into place, and the phones were ringing in the background like a Labor Day telethon. The pace was hectic, but all Dwight was concerned with was a door that, when opened, would transport him right into the thick of it. Looking around, he noticed office doors and bathroom doors. Lo and behold, there it was! The door to the interrogation room was straight ahead. Dwight solves the biggest mystery of his career and, in a few minutes, they will have their man—the elusive Trevor Whitney. Dwight made his approach. He took a deep breath—a focusing breath. Then he heard a whimper in the background. It was the victim's shaken, troubled breathing. She was beaten up and heavily bruised. He could hear the tears like glass hitting the ground. He realized that beyond this point, once he opened up the door, he had to be professional, but, most of all, he had to be careful. It would be like dancing with someone who had no legs. He would have to find a way to get this person to revisit the horrific experience that they had just endured—might as well try to convince a blind person to see a rainbow and describe it. How, in the world, was he going to do that?

Seeing the victims as people doesn't help. Total objectivity allows a detective to see the incident from all angles and not miss a detail. Allowing your emotions to become a distraction is not a good practice if you want to become an expert police detective. It can be dangerous and sometimes cloud a person's judgment. That is one thing. Getting involved with someone who is part of a case is even more taboo. Dwight boasted an impeccable dedication to these policies dictated by the police forces' codes of conduct. Then, with the turn of the door knob, Dwight was forced to "turn over a rock." Dwight has never seen this rock or experienced anyone like Miss Casandra Davis. Garnished by the halo of the single light in an otherwise darkened room, she seemed justifiably frightened. She looked around at the olive-drab-colored walls, marred by smoke stains and years of water damage. The paint in one spot was starting to peel off the walls. Her chair seemed uncomfortable, but the coffee was warm, and everyone, for the most part, was considerate. "Is there someone there?" She called out to the silhouette of Dwight standing in the corner. Dwight thought she was very striking in appearance. In this light, she had a cinematic glow. There were several bruises and lacerations on her arms and one shoulder that he could see. Overall, however, she is in one piece.

They talked about her ordeal, and she agreed that testifying against Mr. Whitney would be best for everyone involved. He wanted to get some background information and take her statement. She would then be free to go. "It says in your report that you are a lounge act for a nightclub called the Lido? Is that true, Miss Davis?" She said nothing—just a slow nod to avoid triggering pain responses that stem from her injuries.

Every now and then, she would wince or shake as the interview progressed. Dwight made his inquiries very delicately, but not because he was trying to get a confession or get her to divulge some detail to the case. She answered every question clearly and concisely. No, it is the way that masculinity naturally behaves in the presence of the feminine. Dwight looked into her eyes for the first time. The honesty of her soul blinded him. He could only peer into her eyes for a moment before having to look away. He tried to be cool and play it straight, but she just looked at him and smiled at his feeble attempts to remain professional while she was being questioned. To describe her would not do her justice. What Dwight saw in that room was a fallen angel. Even with her injuries, she was radiant. Her face was smudged and smeared, but her smile said she was fighting to maintain her composure. She was tired and afraid—it was apparent. Dwight felt it would be wise to establish trust and continue the questioning at a different time. He wanted to give Miss Davis a chance to catch her breath. When he entered, Casandra felt Dwight's manly presence fill the room. He looked into her eyes and saw that she was safe and secure. It had been a while since she had experienced that. It was like a warm blanket and a cup of coffee. Her eyes traced his large, masculine frame. His broad shoulders and square jaw gave him a superhero-like appearance. She wondered what it would be like to touch his hair; he smelled like he had been up all night in the Chicago heat chasing criminals and stopping robberies. Under different circumstances, she would have liked to have gotten to know him. Maybe it was the feeling of sanctuary that he gave her that made her attraction to him overshadow the pain that she had from the bruising and trauma to the head. She was confused and locked those feelings away.

For the moment. She was a bold statement of femininity — a delicate whisper of restraint. A shy girl, she came to Chicago from a small town in Missouri, called Somerset. She was always dramatic and charismatic, but she aspired to emulate the "starinas" and divas who graced the stage and screen. She took dance lessons and voice coaching. By the age of 16, she had honed herself into a powerful performer with no equal. As a youngster, she took a trip with a group of students to New York City to experience sophisticated culture and meet diverse groups of people from all walks of life. This time, she was determined to have the life she always dreamed of. During this time of self-discovery, her parents decided to get a divorce. The court awarded her and her sister to their mother. The mother had now taken to pills and alcohol to deal with the upheaval. Night after night of sickness and neglect led to Cassy's aspiration becoming secondary and soon thereafter, non-existent. What once became a solid foundation for growth and happiness became a chasm of despair, a shelf of sad memories, and broken dreams. In a bold move, at 18, Casandra packed up what little she had and decided that whatever was out there would not come knocking on her door. No, she had to find it for herself. With twenty-seven dollars in her pocket and a black 1984 Ford EXP Turbo, she set her sights on Chi-town— Chicago, Illinois.

The adjustment to city life was a shock to what she was used to. It was like taking a defibrillator to the chest. Many times, the things she witnessed were too much to bear, leaving her breathless and fighting for her survival. She found no time to process what she was experiencing. It all happened so fast. Casandra met a man—a kind man who seemed to know a lot of people and had a certain amount of influence in the "nightlife community." He only went by the name Zackelsbee. Lonely and desperate for a friend, he was the first person to show interest in her, and so they quickly became dependent on each other for survival and warmth. She was working now and managed to save enough to get a one-room flat for her and her new friend to share. She loved performance and fashion. She felt she would be the next big fashion designer, so for fifteen dollars, Cassy purchased an antique brass dress form and started draping. Zackelsbee noticed her working at home. With a bit of coaxing, he managed to get Cassy to try on the clothing piece she had made."Oh no, I couldn't," she refused. "Well, how are you going to find out if it will fit anyone, dear?" Zackelsbe countered. "I will just have one of my friends try it on."

"Oh my, Jesus! Gal, gal, gal! I am your only friend here, and I sure as hell ain't trying on a dress!" Casandra stared at the lifeless dress form and began to imagine what someone would look like wearing it. Zackelsbee was right. The only way to find out what it would look like with someone wearing it is the person wearing it. She tried it on, and it fit very well (as a matter of fact). At that moment, she was reborn and ready to conquer Chicago!

She was no longer a timid little lamb from a small Missouri town. Dwight was surprised to discover she wasn't a she at all. She was indeed born James Raymond Rantor—an effeminate little boy from Somerset, Missouri. It was not until he received much coaxing from his friend, after he moved to Chicago, that he became the Polynesian princess, Casandra Davis. Dwight could only imagine the surprised look on Mr. Whitney's face when he tore off her clothes and found this information out "first hand." Dwight did a full examination of her injuries. He also had a psychologist present to ascertain if there was any (treatable) emotional damage as well.

After carefully looking over the evidence and the testimony of Casandra Davis, Dwight concluded that the perpetrator released Miss Davis because he no longer saw Miss Davis as a woman, someone he would want to make his next victim. The confusion he felt must have caused him to flee the scene and abandon Miss Davis, who was already in a state of confusion herself. He no longer felt the need to continue the subsequent battery, rape, and eventual murder of Miss Davis as he did the other victims. Little did she know that she would be a hero to the women that Trevor Whitney would try to harm in the future. Trevor Whitney could not tell because she was clearly feminine despite her origin. To the untrained eye, there was no reason to believe that she was not a cisgender female. Even her voice had the same depth and resonance as a woman's. Her breasts were soft and perky. Her glassy blues spoke of shyness, although she did not feel ashamed about letting a stranger see her disrobe and stand, totally unclothed, in front of him and others.

Dwight doubted that he would be as obliging to such an examination if the roles were reversed.

After both parties had gotten over the initial shock and awkwardness of the situation, Dwight began to notice a familiar reaction starting to rise in his trousers. He had an erection. He was, after all, a hot-blooded American Male. Dwight thought of nothing else for the weeks following the interview with Miss Davis. He could not confide in anyone about his obsession with her for fear of ridicule or judgment. He knew this scandal could ruin many lives, not just his. He tried to ignore it, but she haunted his every thought and dream. He made up excuses to see her (to gather more information about the Trevor Whitney case, to determine if she knew any of the other victims, to prepare for the trial, and to gather details for her testimony, etc.). He sought her out casually, and then it became an affair. Casandra was only too willing to participate. She wanted him, too. So, Dwight, against his better judgment, started a two-year affair that, eventually, Casandra ended. While he was obsessed with her and all of her female complexities, he could not come to terms with his newfound sexuality. He could not label it, quantify it, classify it, and he could not just surrender to it. He could not, in good conscience, call her his Girlfriend, fiancée, or even acknowledge her in public. With no future and no commitment, she left. She would never be the same again.

As a child, she was able to cope with trauma by blocking out memories of it. With continual abuse, Casandra invented imaginary friends that would take up their cause and be the hero they never had. After the abuse was over, they attributed the end of the torture to his Imaginary superhero. As he got older, the anger never really went away, and his imaginary friends became more violent. They roughed up bullies on the playground. They went around the neighborhood flattening tires and stealing yard ornaments. The older he got, the more dangerous he became. His superhero had a name—Antonio. Antonio followed Jimmy like a big brother, always looking out for Jimmy. He would do anything for his buddy... anything.

Casandra broke it off with Dwight because she did not want the confusion of not knowing if he would leave her once the opportunity for a heterosexual relationship came along. She wanted him to admit that his feelings for her were genuine, valid, and needed his "voice." He recalled how dignified she remained as the tears could not hide that inside her was a storm of emotion coming over her in wave after wave of love and confusion, which turned to anger and confusion. She asked that he should not return to the Lido until he was ready to admit his feelings for her. He needed to validate what they had with a heartfelt commitment. He was simply unable to do it. There was nothing he could say or do except leave without a word. The reports presented in the conference room evoked old feelings. Also, it brought back the familiar churning in the pit of his stomach—relived memories and unresolved issues. Dwight read the signal. He will be confronting these demons in the future—the very near future!

"Dwight!" Dwight noticed that the room had gone silent. Jerry Mack and everyone in the room stared at him. Shaken right out of memory lane, the detective's attention catapulted to the here and now. His worst nightmare had been realized as he looked around at the entire team glaring at him, expecting his input on the information, to which he had not paid any attention. Dwight cleared his throat."Excuse me, everyone. A quick question: Have there been any other cases where the victim wore makeup of this kind? Corresponding colors? similar patterns and textures?" Dwight was proud of himself for pulling that "rabbit out of his hat." Appeased, Jerry Mack directed focus back to the facts of the case, "He is a Caucasian...male...the cause of death was 12 stab wounds— three to the neck—nine to the back. Upon further examination of the body, clothing, and all of its details, pathologists discovered that in the right pocket of the navy overcoat, which the slide clearly shows, they found five thousand dollars in one-hundred-dollar bills. They found an eight-carat diamond solitaire ring in the left pocket, estimated to be worth $62,000.00. These clues are under investigation. If there is any significance, the team gets updated, and the investigation continues with these new clues in play."

Suddenly, as the commissioner was posting the thirteenth slide in the series, a clerk opened the door and handed the commissioner a piece of paper. As the commissioner read it to himself, he looked up at the team of detectives as if to say, "Gentlemen and ladies, this is the day you have all waited for..." His eyes darted around the room. The room notices his silence and waits for any word or expression to clue them in on the announcement he was about to make."Okay, listen up, everyone. We have just received the most disturbing news: a report about the Mayor's Son. His name is David Kinsingsworth. As you may already know, his father is Mayor Carl Kinsingsworth—the Mayor of Chicago.

"David Kensingsworth has been attending Harvard Law School. Teachers last saw him four days ago, but he has not attended classes since. We have contacted all of the shelters in the area. None have reported anyone fitting David's description. We have alerted all of the other precincts to be on the lookout. He has not been identified at any of the hospitals either. An all-points bulletin is issued to keep a lookout for the Mayor's son. We believe he was returning to Chicago to visit his parents, but they have not seen him since he left Harvard. We want to put our top two detectives on this high-profile case, so Dwight, pick a partner and start following up on these leads," Jerry Mack hands a folder to Dwight. Who was going to assist him on this landmark investigation? Jeff Robertson? A likely choice, he is a decorated veteran and a good detective.

Detective Robertson thought Dwight would want his time-tested expertise and experience behind this investigation. Dwight cannot afford to make any mistakes. The media will be right on his heels. They will be reporting on Dwight's every move. The others surely had reasons for Dwight possibly choosing them above everyone else. Dwight's plan, however, took precedence. He knows this decision will alienate him from the rest of the group, but Dwight feels that choosing a relatively new detective would be more advantageous to the case for several reasons. First, inexperienced individuals must work harder to garner respect and attention, so the motivational factor is present. The fact that Dwight wants to choose a woman will appear politically correct to the media and shed a positive light on the force, helping the public warm up to the idea of providing information that could lead to locating Mr. David. The public will be more apt to provide leads, open up during interviews, and verify background information. Second, women have a way of gently coaxing details out of someone during questioning. It may be the warm smile or the nurturing spirit that most women have, naturally. The fact remains, people are more comfortable opening up to female detectives, particularly female victims. Lastly, but not least, let us not forget the time-tested, ever-popular "woman's intuition."

Yes, Dwight was only sure about this one thing..."Sir, I would like to ask Sharon Kastle to be put on this case as my partner." He nodded to the female rookie standing in the corner. "Me? With all due respect, wouldn't you rather put your confidence in someone with a little more experience?"

"Nonsense!"

He walks over to the back of the room, where she is standing, and leans into her left ear, "This is your chance, Ms. Kastle. Do not let me down."

"Miss Kastle's background in paralegal research will prove invaluable in this investigation. I am sure she will give it everything she has."

"Well, we settled that," Jerry Mack announced to the room in approval, "I want you two to get right on it—before someone decides to leak it to the media and we have to issue a statement."

Dwight and Sharon took an unmarked vehicle to the home of the missing Mayor's son. The media had already arrived at the door. The onslaught has already begun. The reporters are feverishly crowding the doorway of the Mayor's home to get a better vantage point. Probing questions and inquiries in hand, they wait for someone to come within the range of the camera. Some of the opening statements made to Mrs. Kinsingsworth are jarring and borderline offensive. Some of the reporters stand in defiance as they call into question the validity of Mrs. Kinsingsworth's parenting skills. Others suggest that David is a child born out of wedlock and decided to run away from home. The reporters use their comments to elicit a reaction from someone inside the house. The door remains unopened. The lady of the house decides to open one of the front curtains gently. Her tears go ignored; no matter what she does, she cannot get them to leave. With every gasp at the question after question firing squad of personal attacks and innuendos, the media showed no mercy.

Like a chivalrous knight rescuing a damsel in distress, our team of Dwight and Sharon pulled up in their shining navy-blue steed. Her eyes turned upward, and she searched for solace as they approached the growing crowd. Her focus fixed on the Duo—now within earshot, she shouts from the front porch for the two to hurry into the house before the madness drives her to say something un-ladylike, risking criticism from her family and (more importantly) her polished peers. She cannot bear to hear her fellow affluent wives say that she is not handling the questioning media vultures with the same elegance and grace that they would have. The men and women of the networks are relentless and continue their pursuit of the "truth." They continue to break down Mrs. Kinsingsworth's defenses. Flashing that winning, plastic smile is now becoming a chore. Yes, Dwight and Sharon's arrival is salvation indeed! Mrs. Kinsingsworth ushers them into the house. She quickly shuts the door. Safe once again in her world, she breathes a sigh of relief. She quickly presents her alabaster arm and gestures toward the main living room. Without a sound, she introduces our two detectives to her comfort zone. Why not surround yourself with things that offer comfort and serenity, and settings that have a calming effect when discussing "ugly things?"

She delicately sits in the room opposite our detectives. She straightens her perfectly coiffed hair and gazes at the two detectives in approval, as if they were her dearest friends. Due to years of political correctness and sugar-coated pretentiousness, Candace barely remembers what friendship is. Skills she gained over her lifetime. She starts under the rock. Then, someone plucks her out of obscurity, cleans her up, and grooms her into a day crawler. Now, she is free to move about on the light side of the rock without fear of being devoured by a predator.

"Hello, I am Candace Kinsingsworth. How may we help you today?"

"Thank you for taking the time out of your busy schedule to answer some questions regarding the disappearance of David, your son."

"Please find him safe and unharmed...please!" She starts to cry, "I will answer all your questions to the best of my ability. Please sit."

Dwight's compliance stems from routine—it makes the host comfortable, and therefore, more willing to answer questions (which are often personal and probing in nature). Generally, the person being interviewed is more cooperative. When an interrogation can be treated like a casual visit, Dwight has learned over the years that more facts reveal themselves, and the more trusting the person being interviewed is in the investigator. The result? More truth is unveiled.

However, Sharon's inexperience is evident, like a flashlight during a game of Hide and Seek—in the dark. She stood. Dwight, with his eyes, subtly motions to the couch. Hint not taken. He gives her a pleading look. This time, she got the hint and sat beside Dwight on the sofa. Mrs. Kinsingsworth offers them a beverage. They politely refuse. They are eager to begin the questioning, getting to the business at hand, the disappearance of her son, David. They start with a few routine questions—physical description, common hangouts, friends, or other family members that he frequently visits. She graciously answers them to the best of her knowledge. One question after another, they asked the distraught socialite, mother of a missing boy, and the Mayor's wife. She is embarrassed by her lack of knowledge about her son's likes and dislikes. It seems a mother should know these details about her son's life.

Underscoring that David's absence could be a cry for attention in a possibly troubled post-adolescent. Dwight does not rule anything out. He searches for the hidden meaning behind what Mrs. Kinsingsworth says to him. His only purpose is to find David. Due to the parents' busy schedules, distance is, to some degree, expected. It sounds like a "rich kid gone bad" story. He wants their love and attention. So, he does his best to try to please them. He goes to great lengths. Doing everything to make them both happy. When the desired response eludes him, he resorts to abnormal behavior. At first, this "dark side" manifests in benign ways (such as poor grades, skipping school, questionable friends, petty theft, etc.). These behaviors are mostly ignored. The parents' response is minimal and temporary. So, he (or she) resorts to more drastic measures. Now, the parents must intervene. This results in harsh feelings of betrayal and abandonment from "Junior," causing many problems for the family.

Years go by. Now, Carl and Candace are resigned to the fact that they are the parents of a "troubled child." They label him the "Black Sheep." David has a stigma attached to his reputation that follows him throughout his life, or (more likely), the child starts to lie. They play a "cat and mouse" game with the parents. Like a creature that crawls across the top of the rock, only to disappear through the gaps. The parents are dismissive and guilt-ridden. The environment becomes toxic until someone disappears. Then, it becomes an investigation. Everyone wonders what went wrong.

This interview has meaning for Dwight. David's story is very similar to his own. Dwight is also a young man who, essentially, raised himself as a child. He sees life as David does—an opportunity to discover life without the benefit of parental supervision or guidance. They were both left to their own devices, experiencing things that he could never discuss with his parents. Mrs. Kinsingsworth is uncomfortable discussing these subjects, even with David. She is a mother who wants nothing to do with her son's curiosity. So, like every good son, David goes to great lengths to avoid them and satisfies his curiosity about such things on his own.

Like any proud mother, Candace only spoke of David's accolades. He is a talented speech writer and political student. He is eager to step into his dad's shoes. The fact that David chose to follow in his father's footsteps makes the Mayor proud. After being accepted to Harvard, he studied International Law and Political Science. He lives on campus with two roommates whom he has never mentioned in conversation. Mrs. Kinsingsworth does not even know their names. Until now, she knows nothing, except that he is doing fine and is enjoying the college experience. She is very polite about her selective ignorance and always smiles when talking about her son. She keeps that same smile even when talking about more sensitive subjects like sexual preference or other unusual behaviors, but this time, it is to mask her uneasiness. These subjects make the visit even more bitter. However, her piety never wavers.

She is matriarchal, yet unnaturally despondent about her dealings with David. Even so, the detectives cannot find anything wrong with the content of her answers, which makes Dwight mildly suspicious.

"Will I be retaining a lawyer?"

"Ma'am, that, of course, is your choice to make, but, as of right now, David is only missing; that is all. Although, because of this case's high-profile nature, having a lawyer handy might be a good idea."

She thanks them for their time and escorts them to the front door. The paparazzi hovers to hear even the slightest bit of conversation, to no avail. Once the door opens, the circus begins again. The endless barrage of probing questions, spoken at deafening volumes, follows the two detectives to their vehicle. Candace Kinsingsworth breathes a sigh of relief that she is not the one selected to "run the gauntlet" of reporters to her car. She turns and slowly closes the door. Dwight and Sharon drive away from the media frenzy and head back to Headquarters. Dwight cannot escape a bittersweet feeling about the interview with the Mayor's wife. She cooperates but offers no tangible insight into David's character or motives. Sharon feels the same, but she chalks it up to procedure. Their presence may have provided comfort and confidence that the investigation will produce a motive, a suspect, and her son. With no leads, the two drive away from the scene. They are drained and disappointed with the results, thus far. Perhaps Jerry Mack has uncovered something while they were away. They turn the corner and arrive at the Precinct Headquarters—just in time.

# Chapter Three-The Lido

"Hey! What's going on here?" Dwight yelled out to anyone within earshot.

"Dwight!" Sharon calls out from the entrance of her office."Where in the hell is Jerry off to in such a Goddamn hurry?"

"Seems there's a break in the Kinsingsworth case. I'll tell you in the car. Let's get out of here!"

On the way to their next destination, Sharon tells Dwight about a report that comes across Jerry's desk as they interview Mrs. Kinsingsworth at her house about a Porsche with license plates matching those of the missing boy. It turns up in the gravel parking lot at the end of an alley. Sharon tries to steady the report in her hands as Dwight rushes to the scene.

"It's a 2024 Porsche 718 Boxster—white with personalized plates—'DRG_CZY'. It is registered to a 22-year-old Caucasian male named David Kinsingsworth. David is 5'11" tall—158 lbs—not found in or near the vehicle."

They roll onto the gravel parking lot, which is reserved only for nightclub customers. The front of the Club can be seen, up ahead, in the alley, from the parking lot. There is a walkway/ramp that leads to the entrance. There is a velvet awning with the nightclub logo embroidered on the front, over the entrance. Two steel doors, secured by a chain and lock, guard the entry into the Club. It seems impenetrable to the two detectives. They will have to get a search warrant to enter the establishment. They will probably need to case the Club for clues and witnesses. "Get on the phone with legal. We are going to need a warrant. Find out who owns the Club, and ask him for an interview."

"Sure thing. What is the name of the Club?" Dwight looks up at the awning and sees the embroidered Gold-thread insignia in the shape of an "L." He knows right away. It is the home of Casandra Davis. The legendary Club... The Lido.

"Why isn't forensics here yet? They left before we did!"

"They can't seem to find the location. It's not found on GPS. They are in the area, and I will guide them to the scene. How did you manage to find this place so quickly?"

"In the meantime, stand by the car. Don't let anyone near this vehicle. It is now a crime scene. I am going to take a look around the perimeter for clues."

He avoids the obvious conundrum. He does not mention that this area is his old "Beat" as an undercover policeman. This is the place where he brings Casandra Davis on several of their dates. Now that he is no longer in the relationship and a newly promoted detective, he can put all this behind him. However, his thoughts betray him. There is still emotional significance for Dwight. He takes his walk and ponders whether letting it be known that he has personal ties to this case would compromise the investigation, resulting in his dismissal from the case and potentially ruining his career. He fears Sharon is picking up on the fact that Dwight's involvement is more than just a case of missing persons. She is smart and intuitive, as expected. Also, she is tenacious. She follows a hunch to its logical conclusion, no matter how small. So, now the cat-and-mouse game shifts onto Dwight's shoulders. Anxious for clues, Dwight decides to wander around. He walks up to the doors of the Club, stops, then turns to head down the alley, around the perimeter fence, and just beyond the entrance of the parking lot. He focuses on the slightest things that catch his eye. Nothing shows up. At the same time, he seizes the opportunity to collect his thoughts and hone in on the present situation. After a while, he comes full circle and heads back toward the abandoned car.

Sharon and forensics pull clues from the scene. Sharon informs Dwight that the keys have been removed from the ignition. They aren't anywhere near the vehicle or the Club. Dwight sees David in his mind. He arrives at the Club and places the keys in his pocket before exiting the vehicle. Conclusion: David is in the car for quite a while before getting out. The gravel is still intact. This suggests that there is no struggle. David leaves the vehicle by choice.

"The emergency brake is on."

"Yeah. David meant to leave it here, but why?"

"I just got off the phone with dispatch. The owner of the Club is Vidal Sassman. He has agreed to meet with us."

"Sassman...an obvious alias—typical of these seedy club-owner types. He might try to exploit the situation for his own personal gain."

"I'll let you handle this one...There he is. He's pulling into the lot now," Sharon nods toward a Black Maybach rolling over the grayish gravel lot. There is a chain-link fence on all sides of the lot, except where it opens onto the road. There is a motorized gate. The gate is monitored 24/7. Where the ramp leads to the entrance of the Club, there is no fence, and it has one security camera. It is only lit at night. One street light illuminates the lot, and colored neon is the lighting choice for the entrance to the Club. Insects prefer the veil of darkness. As Vidal opens the car door and steps out, Dwight notices that the Club owner and the missing boy's mother flash the same Hollywood smile. In both cases, it is a facade to protect what they are hiding in their minds.

As Mr. Sassman introduces himself and shakes Dwight's hand, he cannot shake the notion that he has seen Dwight somewhere before. During the entire search of the vehicle and its contents, Mr. Sassman keeps his gaze on Dwight, thinking it will trigger a memory. He keeps staring. It may unlock the source of the deja vu. Dwight is uneasy in Mr. Sassman's presence. Once again, his past ties with the Lido and its illustrious star, Cassy Davis, clash with the reality of being a protector of the city and a member, in good standing, of the community. Dwight pays close attention to what he says to the club owner and hopes that Mr. Sassman won't expose the "hypocrisy" surrounding our young detective and his ties to Sassman's star performer.

Dwight starts the conversation, and it proves to be unfruitful. The statements given are tainted by Mr. Sassman's desire to promote himself or his Club. Dwight decides to interview Sassman at a later time. He tells Mr. Sassman to make himself available to answer further questions about the case. He is compliant. Dwight and Sharon conclude that David may be a closeted homosexual with an affinity for effeminate, transgender types. However, the Lido is not marketed as a "Gay Club", and Mr. Sassman confesses that all "walks of life" patronize the Club.

Gender illusion, considered an art form by many, attracts people from all races, religions, and socioeconomic backgrounds. It has many incantations in all parts of the world. So, David, our missing Mayor's son, frequents this club. All culpability only lies in the fact that he cultivates an appreciation for a controversial form of art, indigenous to a particular lifestyle, that he may be rubbing elbows with characters of a nefarious nature, and he is definitely mingling outside of his approved social circles. These traits are typical of an affluent, adventurous man of David's charisma, youth, and confidence. Dwight sees a lot of himself in David.

Although Dwight makes sure not to say anything to tip off his partner, Sharon begins to reflect on his actions lately. There is an unexplained distance for no reason. There is an avoidance of her that she doesn't understand. She knows that he is somehow affected by this assignment. Out of professional courtesy, she holds back from acting on her instincts. She thinks about his altered demeanor from the moment they pull into the parking lot, to the walk about alone, with no request for backup. He looks up at the marquis above the entrance to the club, and a nostalgic expression comes over his face. She doesn't have answers. All she does is focus on her job, and with faith that her partner isn't letting her down. He takes a chance and selects her to be his partner. She takes a chance on him that he isn't letting whatever is going on inside his head cloud his vision.

"Sharon, I know I haven't shared many things I do or say with you. I feel like I should clear the air before we continue down the road with this investigation."

"I understand and no."

"What? What do you mean NO?"

"Sir, you chose me to join you on this case, and I never really understood why. The reason is: it's not important. The "why" is not important. I knew that you had been here before when we pulled up in this lot. This case is unlike any other case I have worked on, and something inside me says that you might be the only one among us who can find David. So, don't worry about me. Worry about David, and let's find him. Do what you gotta do. I trust you. You don't have to explain anything. Let's just keep going. I got your back."

"I am afraid that I might be too brash to talk to Mrs. Kinsingsworth about her possibly bi-sexual son—with an obsession for trans-women,"

"So, you're suggesting another visit to his parents' house. Would it be better if I broach the subject with Mrs. Kinsingsworth? Woman to woman?"

"Would you mind? I am never prepared enough to talk to people like David's mother. I don't have the social skills. I always manage to come across as harsh or mean."

"I'll do it."

"Sharon, there are many reasons why I chose you to accompany me on this investigation. None of the reasons have to do with you making a good sidekick or being a woman. However, I hope you understand how valuable these tools can be as a detective."

"Thank you, sir. That means a lot. I have been watching and learning from you since my early days at the Precinct. Your deductive reasoning and pathology are second to none. I am happy to be working alongside you and watching you work firsthand."

"Good, let's bring David Home."

"Yes, we are close to locating him. Real close."

# Chapter Four-The Search for David

"ABSOLUTELY NOT! ARE YOU OUT OF YOUR MINDS? I AM INSULTED THAT TWO PEOPLE OF YOUR POSITION WOULD INSINUATE ANYTHING OF THE SORT ABOUT MY SON! I have half a mind to call my lawyer and sue the department for this slander! You ought to be ashamed of yourselves!" She reaches for a tissue from an ornately decorated porcelain cube. She whimpers into the tissue and takes a moment to regain her composure.

"Ma'am, it's not our intention to cause embarrassment. That is why we want to have this conversation in private—away from the press."

She doesn't respond. She fixates on the tissue in her hands, staring at it."If word of this gets out to them, they will bring their bar-b-ques and set up camp on my front yard. There will be no chance of my getting past this. We will never get back to normalcy. My friends have already begun to distance themselves from my company. They don't come by to visit. They probably will not stand for the embarrassment of getting through the vultures hovering around my front door. I don't blame them...I miss them."

"Does David have any acquaintances? Friends? That accompany him to establishments like the Lido?"

"Lido? What kind of establishment has a name like that?" Mrs. Kinsingsworth draws a blank expression to the follow-up question posed by Detective Kastle, "My David is always a good boy—the very best. He is an excellent student. With all his studying, when would he possibly have enough time to entertain such friends, let alone accompany them to a night club?"

"We have attained his attendance records from Harvard-- the college he attends. They show that David misses quite a bit of school. Does he mention anything about his life apart from his studies in passing? Does he have a person of interest in his life?"

"You mean a girlfriend?"

"Yes, someone that he is having a ..."

"Detective!" she interrupted, "My Husband is out of town. My son is missing. It's mayhem outside, and I am exhausted. Can we revisit this invigorating conversation at a later date and time?"

Dwight, paying respect to the aversion, knows that she is, politely, trying to say: These are things that I need time to process. She is not prepared to address them at this time. They both rise up from the Venetian-style couch and reach the front door. Dwight turns around and looks Mrs. Kinsingsworth in the eye.

"We can contact you early next week."

"Well, I'm not sure. Can I call you? Can I make an appointment? I have appointments all week. Towards the end of the week, I will be free to answer more of your questions."

"Very well then," Dwight said, handing her his card, "My number is there if you need to contact me for any reason. You will receive a call in the next couple of days about another interview. We ask that you remain available if we need more information to help us find your son."

Her response? A slight nod in his general direction and a swift closing of the large wooden door. Dwight and Sharon feel every bit of her passive-aggressive disapproval as they walk past the photographers and media vans to their vehicle. Dwight feels she has little more to offer them about David's life. Still, they don't have enough information on David to form solid leads. They still cannot piece together what happened to the young man, and the media is beginning to clamor for an update.

Dwight sticks with the theory that David is a patron of the Lido. He meets up with trouble while attending the shows. The car is not found in a lake or on the side of a road—abandoned. The keys to the vehicle are missing as well. There are no signs of struggle or traces of blood in the gravel parking lot. All of these point to the fact that David wasn't apprehended against his will. Something lures him away, or he goes willingly. There is one set of tire tracks leaving the gravel lot—apart from Mr. Sassman's Maybach, Dwight's Crown Victoria, and the forensics teams' vehicles, leaving the gravel lot, but they disappear as they get to the alley and head to the main street.

"Are we heading back to the Lido?"

"Yes, I need to find out how the Club is run—how it functions. It may give us insight as to why David went there. Also, it may tell us if he was assaulted there or if he arrived there from somewhere else."

Dwight's mind works against the clock to piece together scenarios that might give them more leads to pursue. The scenarios need to fit the very few clues they have so far. They pull into the Lido parking lot, and Mr. Sassman greets the detectives outside. He guides them into the Club and shows them the layout. Dwight remembers that it looks distinctly different during the daytime. He recalls the days when he was a regular there. It's an industrial space with baroque, cabaret-style decor. Velvet drapes line the stage, and the floor is washed in flat black paint. Tassels and many other details adorn the heavy velvet drapes. Gold embroidery that shimmers in the dimly lit room traces along the edge of the curtains.

The stage is relatively small with intimate tables surrounding it. The tables have red damask table linens with tiny lamps topped with beaded lamp shades on each one. When lit, they cast a warm glow on the faces of the patrons. The stage is round in the front. Staircases in the backstage area lead downward to the dressing rooms. Each performer has their own room. These rooms are private, and a guard at the top of the staircase keeps people from sneaking down to meet the performers. The doors to all of the rooms have locks. The only people with a key are the performers, Mr. Sassman, and the head custodian. Casandra's is the largest of the six rooms that house the different personas. Her room has its sink and vanity. Fans come to the dressing room hoping to "hang out" with the performers. The performers tolerate it until things start to go missing. Souvenirs turn up in the hands of scalpers trying to make a dollar. There is a large, angry man at the top of the stairs with strict instructions to keep all fans and patrons out (but do it gently).

The shows at the Lido have all the glamour and notoriety of any big Hollywood party. Valets park the cars while shirtless bartenders serve the finest spirits and shots. All enjoy the "swirl." That's Casandra's name for the decadent atmosphere in full swing. The overture is heard in the background, signifying that the show is about to begin. Then, one by one, the illusionists glide onto the stage and start to weave their magic on the crowd, who arrive hours in advance, to pay hundreds of dollars for a good table. They do their routines with precision and grace. Costumed and coiffed, they entice and amaze their audience with their effortless portrayal of the feminine mystique.

Casandra Davis is, by far, the most Beautiful and convincing— living proof that beauty has a two-edged sword. Many revered her, but she had her fair share of "fair weather friends" and "haters." She is still one of the most sought-after goddesses in Chicago. She is poetry and mystery with a Polynesian ancestry. When she walks, it's like two praying hands, gently dancing on clouds. Her grace makes every woman she meets envious of her. Her gaze hypnotizes the men. She has a look that says: "Come and get me—if you dare!" She so smoothly slaps someone with a word, cuts them "to the quick" with a glance, and walks away with a Samba in her step. There is no notice of it. She just walks away. She is the Lido's main attraction, and she keeps them coming...again, and again.

All Dwight has to do is close his eyes. He smells the faintly erotic mixture of lilac and cinnamon—her skin. The deepest eyes of ebony fire. She smolders, and the audience feels her heat. Intrigued by the misty-eyed detective, Miss Kastle begins to understand that this is definitely not a routine case. All of the clues, the surroundings, and the players hold weight in Dwight's mind. They carry meaning far beyond the parameters of the case. Perhaps they fade with time, but Sharon notices his emotions, giving him away. Feelings that were dormant for years start to surface as Dwight gazes at the stage and the seating area. He fears that this new flood of nostalgia will compromise his reasoning. While staring at the memorabilia hanging on the wall, his sighs are broken by the female tone of Miss Kastle's greeting of the owner, Vidal Sassman. "Mr. Sassman, thank you for agreeing to meet us again."

"How may I be of further assistance to you and your investigation?"

Dwight knows he must focus on gathering facts to minimize his risk of being tossed off the case because his objectivity has been compromised. This is not the time to reminisce about the past—or maybe it is. With no time to decide how to process his mental regurgitation of a bygone time in his life, Dwight decides to speak.

Mr. Sassman is fixated on the detective for a different reason, forming his agenda. "Say, don't I know you?"

"I don't think so. I would remember if we had met before today, Mr. Sassman."

"...Give me a minute...it will come to me. I never forget a face."

"Mr. Sassman, would it be okay if Detective Hussleman and I asked you a few questions about the car that has been parked in front of your building for the past few days?"

"Okay...sure."

"Do you know who it belongs to?"

"Yes, it belongs to David someone. I know his face, but I don't remember his last name. Everyone just called him 'Hot David.'"

"Was 'Hot David' a regular at the club?"

"I can't tell you that. If I go divulging that kind of intel about my customers—ninety-nine percent of whom prefer to remain anonymous-these doors would close in less than two weeks tops."

"Sounds like you're struggling to keep things afloat financially, Mr. Sassman. We could get a Judge to review all of your records for every business you've run over the last ten years. That might be enough to reveal any flaws in your accounting system. If you want to play 'hard ball', we can play that game. We may discover other things that could be beneficial to know. Cooperating with us now might clear you of all potential charges, conspiracy to commit murder being the big one...you know? We're talking prison time!"

"Spare me the detective mind tricks. I have nothing to do with anyone's son, abandoned cars, or whatever else you're throwing at me. I run a popular night spot...that's all!"

"Don't get too excited. It doesn't look good for you."

"You think I don't know what you're doing? You must see me as some seedy nightclub owner with no brains and no friends. I know people. Get out of here! Get out of my club!"

" We get it—Chicago's best-kept secret and all that. How 'bout this?" Dwight walks up to the Bar owner and grabs him by the lapel. He pulls him in close to make sure that his following words are heard loud and clear, "Once your 'patrons'—if you want to call them that—catch wind that your club was the scene of a crime, they will leave you high and dry anyway. What are you not telling us? Huh? Why are you acting so guilty? I think Miss Kastle and I might feel better continuing this conversation downtown, or maybe we should just add obstruction of justice and withholding information to our list of grievances against you and your establishment."

"Wait, I do know you."

Dwight releases Mr. Sassman. With his back against the wall and, at a safe distance away from Dwight and Sharon, he fixates on the detective's facial features. Suddenly, a light bulb comes on in his mind.

"Yeah, I know your face! I only saw you once, but she always talked about you. You're the one. You're him." Vidal said as he stood with his back against the wall.

"You said 'she'?" Miss Kastle's inquiry was indicative of her excellent sleuthing skills.

"We're going..." Dwight grabs Miss Kastle's arm and quickly heads for the door, before the club owner can complete his thought. "Cassy mentioned how much she was..."

As they leave, Dwight turns around and looks at the club owner eye to eye, "It seems that the only way to get the information we need is with the help of the district court! We'll be in touch!"

The whirlwind confuses Sharon. She is frustrated. This did not feel like proper procedure. Detective Hussleman is not handling this situation in his usual calm and collected manner. Dwight notices the insane expression in her eyes. Dwight says nothing. He just stares at the road ahead. He is searching for the words before the awkward silence becomes too long. Dwight seeks an escape from culpability and shame. His partner's validation that her hunches about him are correct seems imminent. His objectivity is compromised. He turns to look at her. Then, he looks at the road again. Again, he looks at Sharon. He was still not sure. He drove onward. All he knew was that without any information from the missing boy's family and no eyewitnesses on the night of his disappearance, they were back at square one. This was the conclusion that Sharon also shared with Dwight. She decided that to get to the bottom of the investigation and solve the mystery of the disappearing Mayor's son, she would have to table her personal inquiries for the time being. She saw Mr. Hussleman's face and knew immediately that unless she said something to diffuse the tension, Dwight would spend the whole car ride obsessing about her opinion of him, not prioritizing the Mayor's missing son.

"We need to keep the area of the car and the surrounding lot secure, at least a fifteen-foot radius in case we need to revisit this scene to look for more clues and to protect the vehicle from possible vandals. I'm going to call for a 72-hour watch over the site. Two uniformed officers should cover it. They can take four-hour shifts." Sharon said.

"Yeah, sounds good."

The pain from the spider bite was still pulsing in the detective's leg. It seemed as if the wound was beginning to worsen, and Dwight was feeling feverish. Beads of sweat began to run down his face. Dwight would grit his teeth in pain each time he flexed his thigh. He didn't want to draw attention away from the facts of the case, but he could no longer ignore the degenerated flesh, causing his slacks to darken with a stain. While Sharon summoned the police, Dwight changed his course and headed for Community General Hospital.

As they pulled into the emergency room, Dwight, determined that he wasn't going to let this little creature get the best of him, deduced that he should let the doctors do their job and he should do his. So he sat on the table, and the RNA patched up what had turned into an infected, weeping hole that was swollen and black.

The shot they gave him began to ease his pain, and he drifted onto a tangent about his wife, Misty. She was so beautiful in the half-light of the moon. Dwight saw the vision of moonlight dancing on Misty's body. He said a small prayer asking for her protection and resolved to call her once they got a break. Gently, Dwight let out a humorous chuckle. There are no breaks. Even with the pleasant thoughts of Misty and the day's events so far, a small wave of disappointment came over him because it had been almost five and a half hours, and still no new leads, no significant clues, no real suspects, nothing.

They didn't have any clear leads in the case. They didn't even have a body or motive. It won't be long until the media starts turning this into a circus and starts making a mockery of the Chicago police force and its investigative team. The only thing they knew about the case of the missing mayor's son was that he had driven his car to the Lido, where he parked it and then "disappeared". The rain and the next day's sun had all but washed away the tracks leading in any direction to or from the gravel parking lot and onto the street. Sharon waited in the holding area while Dwight had his pants down in Emergency Room One. She paced and waited for the doctors to patch him up. Sharon thought any minute detail that escapes notice could be the ground-breaking clue they have been waiting for. "Well, it hasn't been much of a morning so far," Dwight mused as he exited the examination room.

"Are you gonna be okay?"

"Yeah. It's just a spider bite. Got a little infected. You know. The usual."

"Well, if it weren't for the two dock workers finding that corpse at the end of the pier this morning, there wouldn't have been anything for me to write home about at all," She said, followed by a welcome laugh.

As Dwight drove away from the hospital, he silently shared her amusement. He thought to himself, what a coincidence that the body of someone from his past should turn up dead, and a high-profile member of an affluent Chicago family should be reported missing. It's a stretch, but what if the two were connected somehow? After all, Jimmy Rantor, a.k.a. Casandra Davis, performed at the same club where David Kinsingsworth's car had been abandoned. Unfortunately, the connection of the two stops there. "Was Jimmy Rantor ever officially reported missing?" Dwight asked, hoping that Miss Kastle could follow his train of reasoning and help him see a correlation between Miss Davis and Mr. Kinsingsworth, "No eye witnesses? Other than the two dock workers?"

"No, and we already went over the dockworker's statements. They didn't see the body get dropped off, and no one else was at the pier before their arrival. They were just going to their normal work day."

"Was there any security camera footage or security officers on duty who can testify that there was no activity on the pier before the two men went to work and saw the object bundled and abandoned at the end of Pier 14?"

"The security agency that looks after Pier 14 during the 11 pm to 7 am shift said that they did not have a guard on duty last night. Their contractual obligation for that area is for Monday through Friday overnight. Since last night was Sunday, there was no one on duty."

"No cameras?"

"None."

Recollecting the facts of the case, Dwight asked Sharon a barrage of questions, all aimed at triggering some connection between the missing mayor's son and the Lido's star performer, Casandra Davis.

"All we know about the victim," Dwight said, "is that he was a street punk named Jimmy Rantor."

"His birth name is probably James. James Rantor—Street Punk," offered Sharon. She wondered if now would be a good time to confront Dwight about his strange behavior regarding certain aspects of the case, like whenever mentioning Casandra Davis.

"Before we go any further with this investigation, Sharon, there is something I have to tell you," Dwight stated as a preemptive effort to acknowledge his partner's suspicions about his past.

"Sir, if I gave you the impression that I had any suspicions that you knew Miss Davis..."

Sharon stopped herself, trying to show Dwight that his confession was unnecessary, and that a confession like this to her could put her in an awkward position and force her to consider removing Dwight from the case. She needed his knowledge, wisdom, and experience to solve this disappearance.

Dwight felt compelled to clear the air. As a friend and faithful partner, Sharon felt that Dwight's admission of his connection to Miss Davis was a sign that he was working through an issue in his past. Indeed, if he does not come clean about his involvement with her, it could stifle his thought process and deductive reasoning, thus opening him up to make all kinds of mistakes. No, it was vital that she not only heard what Dwight had to say but also held it in trust and did not tell anyone."C'mon, let's grab some coffee, my treat."

They drove to a diner in the middle of town and sat in a back booth—dimly lit. Dwight told her the whole story about Trevor Whitney, the two-year affair, and Casandra's decision to break off the relationship, as well as how he felt about her and how it had changed his life. He still had unresolved feelings of guilt and shame, as well as feelings of love and respect for her and what she had been through. He talked about the lifestyle, the different characters he had known while dating her, and shared stories of the good times he had with Casandra. He told Miss Kastle everything, that if he ever had the chance to be with her again, he wouldn't hesitate. Then, Dwight met Misty, his wife, and they had two children together. He would be conflicted if he were ever to choose between a life with Casandra or his life with Misty and their kids.

Sharon was moved by his story, but played the objective therapist well. Her comforting smile put our dedicated detective at ease. He could open up to her and unload his burden of heavy emotion with impunity. He knew that he could trust his partner to keep his confession in confidence. At least until they are able to solve this case. A wave of empathy came over Sharon when she realized that lying slain on Pier 14 last Sunday, was a big part of Dwight's life, and that this case means more than just a "feather in the cap" of police commissioner Jerry Mack. Sharon couldn't help but feel that Dwight's confession affected the gravitas of the case. There was a deep-seated motivation to solve it, more so now than before. She also felt that there was a correlation between the missing mayor's son and the Illusionist Miss Davis. Not only that, but she felt an unseen feeling of obstruction that she had not felt before, and it seemed to be lifted. The metaphysical energy needed to solve this case had finally begun to flow.

"You there? Can you hear me?" It was Jerry Mack calling Dwight. Dwight put him on speaker. "We got a call from the owner of the Lido—a Mr. Vidal Sassman. He is asking for you specifically, Dwight. Head on down there and talk to him, Will ya? See if he has anything that he can contribute to the investigation and if he wants to make a statement. Dwight, we are running out of time and options. In a few days, the media will start clamoring for a suspect, and, I hope, when that happens, we can give them one. Get it?"

"Got it. Thanks, Mack."

"It's not a problem," Sharon volunteered. "I will go over the car for clues with forensics, and you can get Vidal's statement. He is probably going to want to know what happened between you and the Polynesian Princess we found wrapped up on Pier 14," Sharon said in a low tone—one that she thought made her sound like a "hard-line" investigator—tough and emotionless.

"Hey! Have some respect for the deceased. We are here to help them and their families find the peace they need to move on amid tragedy and possibly keep it from happening to another hapless victim in the process," Dwight reprimanded.

"Sorry, Dwight, I didn't want to make light of the victim's death, especially since this one has meaning for you. That's the last thing I want to happen," Sharon apologized, deciding that she would save her authoritative voice for a more appropriate time in the future. In light of Sharon's knowledge, Dwight wasn't sure if she was being passive-aggressive when she said they should be careful now that Dwight is connected to the victim. No matter. He confided in her for a reason. He chose her to be his partner for a reason—even if that reason turns around and ends up biting him in the ass.

Dwight turned and gave Sharon a forgiving nod. But his mind was transfixed on a thought that flew by him and was circling its way back. Something Sharon said triggered him into a conclusion he hadn't thought about until now. He was preparing to pull into the Lido's parking lot ahead of the forensics team. The Porsche was still parked and looked as if it remained undisturbed. Mr. Sassman had gentlemen stationed at the front door of the nightclub, waiting to escort our investigator into the main dance floor and stage area. The gentleman politely asked if Dwight wanted a beverage, to which Dwight respectfully declined. He found a bar stool at the end of the shiny countertop, gently hoisted his body onto it, and waited for Mr Sassman to enter the room.

"I am sorry that we didn't get the chance to finish our interview the other night. You left in such a rush; I wasn't sure why," Mr Sassman said as he approached Mr Hussleman at the bar. He offered his hand in a gesture of truce and expected Dwight to shake it, to which Dwight, again, respectfully declined. "Mr. Sassman, I wanted to ask you some more questions about the owner of the Porsche that is parked outside. Do you know how long it has been there? Is it abandoned?" Dwight didn't want to overwhelm him with too many questions at the same time.

"I will do my best to answer them. The car belongs to David, a regular at the club. He came in on the weekends. We met a few times, but I don't really know him. David and his friend were weekend warriors. You know, just another face in the crowd, a customer. The car has been there for four days now. One of my hostesses says that Mr. David left with Miss Cassy Davis in her vehicle and hasn't returned. That's why I thought you were here. To find out what happened to Casandra. Since you two knew each other, who better to head up an investigation into her disappearance."

"No, sir, we are following up leads on a different investigation. Please answer the question: Do you think Mr. David may return for his vehicle?" Dwight was insistent for two reasons. The answer will help him determine whether or not David is alive. Also, it will help determine if Mr. Sassman had a hand in any foul play regarding David Kinsingsworth's disappearance.

"Then why you? Why ask you to conduct this investigation? Any man in Blue can ask me those questions. No, you, sir, are here for a reason. According to the same hostess at the front foyer, David came to the Lido almost every weekend with a college buddy. The two had a blast! Both young and good-looking, they garnered a lot of attention. Some good, some not so good. However, I wouldn't consider them "trouble makers." They were never asked to leave the club. In fact, everyone liked them. After a while, Mr David would be seen talking with the performers. One in particular, our star— Casandra Davis, seemed to have captured his fancy. Once her night's performances were finished, she would invite Mr. David and his buddy to hang out with her in her dressing room. David would leave with Casandra, and his wingman would drive the Porsche back to where they were staying."

"Why didn't his friend drive the vehicle home last Saturday night?"

"I wondered that myself," Mr Sassman empathized," So I asked our hostess if Mr. David's friend was with him this weekend? She said neither of them saw the show. She said that David came to the Wednesday night open mike and had a couple of drinks. When she told him that Cassy Davis wasn't performing that night, he left. However, Mr. David did not drive his own car, but took a taxi. David's rendezvous with Casandra took precedence over the safety of his expensive sports car. I imagine if anything happened to it, his insurance would cover it. And it's posted in the parking lot that the vehicle will be towed after five consecutive days. It's only been four days. Ain't that a thing!"

"I assure you, Mr. Sassman, that once we have gathered all of the evidence we need from this crime scene, we will remove all of the caution tape and have the car towed to where we store vehicles as forensic evidence."

"Is that all you need from me then?" Mr. Sassman said in a way that hinted to our Detective that he should find his star performer before next weekend or risk filing the the disappearance of David Kinsingsworth in a cold case file, archived until the end of time.

"I would like access to Miss Davis' dressing room. Since she would invite Mr. David down there to visit, there might be clues that could lead us to Mr. David or someone who knows what happened to him."

Mr. Sassman directed our detective to a darkened corner of the backstage area. He pointed to the descending staircase and turned on the light for him. Dwight took each step slowly. He held onto the rail, bolted to the cinder block wall, which was painted a slick black. The smell was of old cigarettes and fresh paint. He felt an energy rise to greet him, and he lowered himself, step by step, into a world few get the privilege to see. This was her private world. The room where one person goes in and, after a while, a new person emerges, a metamorphosis occurs. A person full of color, glamour, and life assumes the role of the glamour doll, the dancing queen, or the comic. This is the "cocoon". This is where human butterflies are made. There was a green room where performers waited until they took the stage. It had beverages and snacks. There was closed-circuit television to watch what was happening above ground, complete with sound. There were thirteen dressing stations and four private dressing rooms, all of which were kept locked at all times. The only people possessing a key to those rooms are the performers and Mr. Sassman's janitorial staff.

The staff kept the dressing rooms clean, and Dwight didn't notice anything that would send up a red flag in this investigation or anything that appeared to be a smoking gun. Upon each door was the name of each performer, and below it, a star made of glitter. He walked further and saw the door marked "CASSY." He stopped and pondered the implications of what might be beyond the door. His anticipation turned into apprehension. "It's just feathers and makeup," He thought to himself, "What else could it be?" Dwight tried to turn the knob, but the door wouldn't open. He didn't have the key. He turned around, and staring him in the face was a dark figure about Dwight's height and build. Dwight was startled at the unannounced man sneaking up on him. Then he saw the bucket behind him and a mop in his hand.

"I am Antonio. The boss said that you might need a key." Antonio reached into his faded navy work pants and pulled out a shiny silver key. "This is the key to Miss Cassy's dressing room. You will need it to open the door and look around."

"Thank you. By the way, would you mind if I asked a couple of questions, as someone who regularly has access to this area? Have you noticed anything out of the ordinary? In particular, the last four days?" Dwight asked.

"Besides the mess they leave behind? Nothing. I haven't noticed anything."

Antonio replied. Dwight felt that it was the janitor's obligation not to divulge any information without the approval of his boss.

Dwight redirected the questions."Your boss says Miss Davis would entertain patrons in her dressing room. Doesn't that go against your policy denying access to the dressing area by anyone other than the performers and their assistants?"

"Yes, sir, we are very strict about that. It keeps theft down to a minimum. Makes it easy to find out who stole from whom. However, if some are allowed in the dressing against company policy, that is something that has to be taken up with security—not janitorial. The clean-up crew only works on Saturdays and Sundays."

"Do you clean the locked rooms?"

"No, sir. Just the Green room and lounge area. Each performer is responsible for keeping their private dressing room clean. However, Miss Davis had a separate cleaning person for her dressing room."

"So, she would show up, and you would let her in. She cleaned the room, and you would lock it up after she left?"

"Yes, sir."

"Did she clean after every show?"

"Yes, except lately she hasn't been doing Saturday nights. She would wait and clean up on Sunday."

"Do you know the name of this dressing room assistant, and how I might get in touch with her to ask a few questions about Miss Davis?"

"Sorry, sir, I only know her first name, Carmen."

"Well, that's a start." Dwight said as he made his way to Casandra's dressing room. Once again, he felt a weight holding the door closed. It was his own apprehension that was trying to stop him from taking the key and putting it in the hole, and he did it gently. The light had been left on. A glowing, soft light emitted just enough to illuminate the important details of the room. The single incandescent bulb was dim. Dwight concluded it had been left on for some time. A long table with barely enough space for the items used to create that iconic image--the one that transfixes the audiences, night after night--remained undisturbed. The walls were a rich China red, with analogous colored fabrics draped to add dimension to the decor. There were photos on the wall, and on the mirror were momentos of special moments on stage. Most pictures were of her posing with different people who frequented the club.

Dwight noticed that none were taken in the dressing room, except one. Tucked halfway underneath a napkin on the table in front of the mirror was an overexposed picture of a young man posing with our star. She had her arms around his neck and leaned in for a kiss on the cheek. His eyes were closed, indicating that this was a completely candid shot and that the subject may have been intoxicated when the picture was taken. He was shirtless and standing in front of the clothing rack. Dwight suspected that this was our missing Mayor's son, David Kinsingsworth. With no one looking, he pocketed the photograph and took one last look at the dressing room. He locked the door knob and exited.

"Did you find what you were looking for, Mr. Hussleman?" A voice came from the main room once again. It was Mr. Sassman. Dwight approached the club owner.

"I have everything I need. Please remain available to answer any questions that come up as we gather more facts pertaining to this case."

"What about the Queen Casandra Davis? What About my Star?" Mr Sassman shouted at Dwight as he exited the building. Outside, Sharon was gathering evidence from the vehicle. Members of the forensics team performed various tasks to find clues that could expedite the investigation. She saw him exit the building and stopped to meet him. Dwight was clearly upset. She felt like Dwight had found something. Was it something he could confide in her about? She quickened her pace so that she could come up alongside him and match his gait. He was breathing heavier, and his stride was considerable. She could barely keep up.

"Did the club owner have anything useful? Did you get his statement? Did he have any facts to contribute?" Sharon asked. Sharon's breathing becomes heavier as they arrive at their official police business vehicle —a navy blue Crown Victoria with license plate CHPD 2375. Dwight opened the driver's side, and Sharon instinctively opened the passenger side. She still had no response to her inquiry. Dwight's face lost all expression as he glanced over at his partner. She matched his glance and started to enter the car."I'll explain everything...get in," Dwight fervently requested.

The two doors slammed, and they drove away, leaving the club, David's car, and the forensics team to their work."Okay, so, where are we heading?" Sharon asked. Her tone was urgent, but objective.

"Back to Mercy," Dwight responded.

"The Hospital? Did you leave your phone there? Is there something we missed?"

"Yeah, the coroner's report." Sharon's curiosity had been piqued. Just then, a call came in from Jerry Mack. He was at the precinct. Dwight silenced the call as he pulled into the Hospital drive. Walking towards the revolving door, Sharon stops him and asks him to let her in on the hunch.

"Sharon, do you remember the meeting room this morning and the first slide of the victim that was found on the pier?" Dwight stopped and turned towards her, right in front of the doorway, as people entered and exited the building. He wasn't sure whether he was heading in the right direction, and if Sharon could follow his train of thought, she would be able to validate his suspicions, thereby having their first real lead.

"Yeah, yeah, Jimmy Rantor," Sharon replied. So far, so good.

"Do you remember how J. Mack described the victim to everyone in the room?" Dwight continued.

"...um yeah sure. Caucasian male, age twenty-two, wearing makeup, five thousand dollars in one pocket and an 8-karat diamond ring in the other pocket..."

"Correct! Keep going! What else did he say?" Dwight insisted, knowing Sharon was trying to follow along, but she didn't quite understand what she was to conclude. Dwight patiently waited for the epiphany. "Okay, let's see," She thought out loud, "He was wearing a navy blue trench coat and heavy makeup with mascara running down his face. The mascara was messed up before they dumped the body in the rain, which suggests to me that the victim was crying before being slain and taken to the pier."

"Okay, think about what you just said." He waited. Nothing was connecting. Sharon tried hard to tap into Dwight's hints, but his payoff eluded her."Sorry, I got nothin'," Sharon said, beginning to doubt her sleuthing skills."There is no way the body on the pier was Jimmy Rantor, a.k.a. Casandra Davis. At least not the Casandra Davis that I knew and loved."

"Dwight, please. This is not the time for riddles!" Sharon raised her voice in frustration. She was more disappointed in her lack of deductive reasoning than Dwight's lack of transparency: "Did you just send Jerry Mack to voicemail?"

"Yes, I did. Don't try to change the subject. Part of being a good detective is learning to find clues where there are none. You start to look at things differently. You see things not for what they are, but for what they are not. You look for inconsistencies and body language, breaches in manner and protocol, etc. Do you see what I mean?"

"I think so. There was a breach in procedure this morning. Jerry did not disclose any facts from the coroner's report during the meeting. A report with clues that could help point to a suspect."

"Right!" Dwight was proud of his apprentice for remembering."I just thought that the call interrupted his presentation, and he wasn't able to go over the details of the coroner's report," Sharon added. "Or maybe there wasn't a coroner's report at all," said Dwight. "I am not sure what the reason would be. I don't know. My instincts usually have a beat on things like this. Maybe they didn't want to spend the money to do an autopsy on a street punk found at the end of the pier when the attention shifted to the Mayor's son. All available funds were probably redirected to the investigation of David's disappearance."

"Dwight, I think that's a reach." Sharon's role had switched to devil's advocate. "If what you're saying is true, then any facts regarding the victim found on the pier could be inconclusive."

"This case would have been filed as a 'cold case' anyway—swept under the rug. An autopsy would have just been a waste of time and tax dollars."

"That's true. So, the facts were quickly disclosed, and it was just gonna be left open but not pursued." Sharon was now catching up to Dwight's reasoning.

"Which makes me wonder, since headquarters was unaware that the two cases may be linked, we should let them know our direction and ask them to perform an autopsy. To do that, you need probable cause. Some reason, important enough to spend the money on Jimmy's autopsy."

"I've got one," Dwight was about to put the icing on the cake, "Jerry Mack described the race of the victim on the pier as a Caucasian male. How did I describe Casandra to you?"

"Oh My God!!" Sharon could not contain her bewilderment that she missed the fact that the race of the victim indicated that it was not Jimmy Rantor. "You said that she was of Polynesian descent. So, that means that the body on the pier can't be Jimmy Rantor," Dwight didn't say a word. He got his payoff.

Dwight's silence was to let his assistant digest the implications of what he was suggesting. If the body from that morning did not belong to Jimmy, then it is possible that Mr. Rantor was still alive, and also Miss Davis. It also meant that Casandra and David may still be alive and together somewhere. Dwight and Sharon discussed all of the ramifications of ordering an autopsy on the body that was found on Pier 14. Who was it? Why was there an effort to dismiss this as a cold case? What actually happened to David Kinsingsworth and Casandra Davis? Yes, the epiphany had knocked our detectives, once again, down to square one.

"It's still suspect that a body gets dumped on a pier about the same time that the Mayor's son, David, goes missing," said Sharon, grasping for a new direction to take this investigation.

"It does, and now we have two missing people and a dead body," Dwight added.

At that moment, Sharon got a call from the precinct. It was Jerry Mack. Dwight could hear his voice yelling into the phone. There were a few choice words aimed at Dwight for not answering his phone calls. After about two-and-a-half minutes of ranting, Jerry Mack revealed some facts from forensics about the abandoned Porsche. "The car was clean of fingerprints," Jerry began, "The battery was intact. If David had the key, the car would have had no problem starting up. That indicates that he intended to come back for the vehicle. The car was locked, and the keys were nowhere to be found. The interior was spotless except for a wad of chewing gum in a wrapper and a broken silver house key in the ashtray. The key had no markings other than the brand "Master Lock" embossed at the top of the key on both sides. The rocks from the parking lot were not embedded in the tread of the tires, which says that once he got there, the car never moved. He didn't leave and come back multiple times—just once. There were no scratches on the paint and nothing in the trunk. The engine was half full of premium unleaded—no surprise. According to GPS, several calls of considerable length were made from the vehicle. There were two noteworthy calls: A 12-minute call to Cajam and a 22-minute call to Kyltem—we think they might be nicknames on his contacts list. Contact lists are usually synced to the car, but no cell phone was found near the vehicle."

"Thanks, Jerry. Do you think it will be possible to have a DNA test done on the body that was discovered on Pier 14?"

"What? The street kid? What the hell?" Jerry Mack was not keen on the idea. Too much time has passed. "I can make some calls to the morgue and see what they did with his body. What's his name? Jimmy. I'll let you know."

" We suspect there may be a link to the Mayor's Son's disappearance."

"Oh! I can't wait to hear this one. No problem. Also, I will have a copy of the report on your desk when you get back to Headquarters," Jerry said as he hung up the phone.

"Where do you wanna start?" Sharon asked, understanding that the facts coming in needed to be analyzed, processed, and tied into the rest of the clues to paint a complete picture of what happened to our missing Mayor's Son and Miss Davis.

"Well, I think we have gathered all we can from the abandoned Porsche and the Lido," Dwight said, sifting through the scenarios in his head. "We'll start with David. We know that he may have been, at the very least, bi-sexual. He has been skipping classes to come to the Lido on the weekends, and he has a penchant for Polynesian Drag Queens. We need to know if he had any friends who may have seen him around, any places that he frequented to eat or do homework."

They pulled into the precinct and went directly to Jerry Mack's office. They had a meeting to discuss what they knew to be true about the case. Behind closed doors, to convince Jerry that he needed to order a DNA test on the victim discovered on Pier 14, Dwight had to let Jerry Mack in on his affiliation to Casandra Davis, the two year affair and the fact that Mr. Sassman knew Dwight from going to the club going on dates with Miss Cassy and his two year relationship with her. Jerry agreed to keep it a secret if it didn't come out in the press. However, Dwight did not divulge his hunch that the body from the pier might be our missing Mayor's Son. He thought he would let the DNA test reveal that fact independently. Jerry took them to the evidence room, where they found the broken key and a photo of David's Porsche parked at the Lido. A map showing the locations of David's parents' house, the pier, and the nightclub was connected with a string and marked with push pins of various colors. Sharon marked two more places—Harvard Law School and David's Fraternity House. That's where they told Jerry Mack they were heading next. "Before you go, you'll both want to be here in the morning for the press conference," Jerry suggested that the two should be present, which was not received well.

"You called a press conference for tomorrow morning?"

"Well, I didn't, but, the Mayor called the press conference to let the media know that we are working hard on the case and that he has every confidence that Chicago's finest will find the suspect or suspects and bring them to justice," Jerry stated it like a speech; like he was the POTUS giving the keynote address at the White House, "So make sure that you are dressed appropriately and on your best behavior. Got it?"

"Okay, okay. Then, after the press conference, we'll head to Boston to get some background on the 'golden boy' David."

"See you tomorrow." Jerry Mack left the room. His demeanor seemed more at ease. Dwight felt he had given Jerry Mack enough reassurance to sate the commissioner's anxiety. Finally, he could take a moment and look at the clues and the evidence with a little more insight. He stood in front of the corkboard, which displayed all the case photos. He was silent and deep in thought—a man of few words challenged by too few clues.

"We can't be sure about any of this until we get the DNA test results back," Sharon said as she carefully approached Dwight at the board. Dwight's concentration broke. He realized what she was saying was right, and it was time to get some needed sleep before the press conference in the morning.

"When was the press conference again?"

"8 am."

"Okay, I'm heading home. Do the same and get some good rest. We have to kiss babies and shake hands in the morning."

"A fate worse than death," Sharon added as they both shared a laugh, "Hey, maybe sometime you could tell me your story about you and Miss Davis. I have so many questions."

"That's why I don't really talk about it. I told you most of it. I'm not really sure why I did it. Or why I want it back. Go home, Sharon, 8 am comes really early."

"I'll bring the coffee."

# Chapter Five-The Learning Curve

A flash of lightning and a clap of thunder illuminated the night. A strike of a match touching the wick of a lavender votive candle, then a creme colored, vanilla-scented votive. Another flash, and the rain droplets could be heard beating against the roof of the small apartment. Two shadows heard breathing heavily and whispering laughter in the night, paid no attention to the storm brewing outside. Even in the sound of wave after wave of heavy rain, you could faintly make out lips seeking out lips and coming together. Touch begets touch and sigh begets sigh. Casandra slides the palm of her hand down the curve of David's back. He surrenders to her touch. She looks at him and sees her future. Nothing matters except this moment. The wind howls in protest, but they press on. Discovering new patches of love covered in warmth on a cold, rainy night. He holds her as they turn. She looks up at him and searches his eyes. He looks at her in the light of the flickering candles and the romantic, unceasing rain. He kisses her, and she closes her eyes to join with him in this moment and the next.

Suddenly, a frantic beating at the door interrupts the two as the frenzied vibration of a fist repeatedly banging against the door of Casandra's studio. A man's voice was pleading behind the triple-locked door. The pounding and the storm could not disturb the throes of passion. They couldn't hear anything for the world was tuned out and secondary. Casandra opens her eyes to see if David could hear the faint sound coming from beyond the living room and out in the hall. It sounded like pounding. David ignored the assault on the door and the snap in the door's lock. He takes his manly fingertip and thumb, gently touches Cassy's chin, and turns it back towards him. Another flash of lightning and a clap of thunder broke through the clouds. Casandra was disturbed this time, but David comforts her, saying it is only the rain. Who could it be so late in the evening? Not one second more, and splintered shards of wood burst from the door jam of her apartment, and a lumbering figure drenched in rain and breathing heavily stood in the doorway of her bedroom. The force of the door opening and the draft that flooded the tiny apartment blew out the candles so the two could barely make out the figure standing there, now in their bedroom doorway, silent and holding something in his hands. David continued to lie on top of her so that whatever happened, he could protect her, as there was no time to stand up, let alone get dressed.

For an eternity, the dark, ominous figure just stood silent and stared at the two lovers bathed in the half-light of the rainstorm. Another flash of lightning. This time with no thunder. And just as quickly as he appeared there, the mysterious dark figure was gone. Whatever was in his hand was dropped to the floor. Casandra knew that it had to be none other than Kyle Templeman. Why did he show up without calling first? How did he know that David was here? What could he have wanted so late on such a dark and dreary night? Just a few moments later, the dark figure reappeared. Kyle had come back. Now the object in his hand was pointed and curved. Now breathing heavier and moving quickly. Cassy shouted, "Kyle!" David's body went limp. Warm liquid began saturating the sheets. The darkness veiled the color, but it was warm and viscous. Another bounce of the bed, and David's eyes went lifeless with an expression that could only mean one thing: they were being attacked.

The assailant penetrates the back of him again, blood starts to run out of his mouth, and she is now drenched in it. The sheets are dark from all of the blood draining from David's body. David's life force, spilling onto the floor of the bedroom, was leaving his body. She could see the assailant's face with every flash of lightning and make out who it was. She realized that she could not scream because the murderer would know that she was still alive. Feigning death, she closes her eyes and thinks of David. Was there any chance he would be alive when she opens her eyes? Casandra searches for a heartbeat, but there is just a lifeless body getting heavier by the second. She wanted to scream out in horror, but a couple of the stabs had grazed her neck. The pain was too great to utter any sound. She had no choice but to lie there. As she lay, she felt the blade that was penetrating David's back and body come through and slightly pierce her flesh. She was bleeding too. She felt every single point plowing through David and piercing her. His head could not stay upright and rested next to hers on her shoulder. His eyes were still open. The rain had stopped, and she saw bright flashes, not from lightning or candles, but from a phone camera. The murderer was taking pictures of David. The disgust welled up in Casandra and she began to heave.

Casandra felt lightheaded and her eyes began to get heavy. However, before she passed out, one last flash of lightning illuminated the room, and she saw the face of the attacker. It was as plain as day. She was too weak to move and just lay there with David. He was so heavy now. She could barely take a full breath. Nauseous and weak from blood loss, she was too tired to keep her eyes open and slowly drifted to sleep. There were still thumps and bumps from noises in the apartment, and she could hear objects shattering in the background, but she was helpless to do anything. She could hear someone faintly calling her name, but could not respond. Barely awake, she musters up enough strength to put her arm around David as if to ease his passing and to tell him she loved him. Although she couldn't see anything, she could feel the gaps in the skin on his back and the thick, warm liquid bathing them both. She wanted to cry, but was unable. Mentally, she was preparing to say goodbye. She prepares for her inevitability and closes her eyes.

# Chapter Six-Bullets from Heaven

Press conferences can seem unnecessary and trite, but they can also be a valuable tool for flushing out a suspect or lead that could help solve a complex case. The Mayor held this press conference to reassure the public that the case is being actively investigated and resolved. Mr. Kinsingsworth also wanted to encourage anyone to come forward with any information that might lead to the identification of a suspect. Dwight and Sharon stood on the sidelines waiting for the reporters to finish. They were anxious to get back to hunting for clues.

Just as the Mayor approached the podium, shots rang out. Immediately, everyone hit the ground in horror. The confusion sent the police into action. Pulling their guns and securing the area, their awareness was heightened as they took control of the situation. Every second and every sound mattered. Four members of the security team immediately ran to the Mayor, and two to the Commissioner. The other officers began to scout the area, looking for a gunman hidden in a room or vehicle. People were scattered and running in all directions. Dropping notes and tripping over folding chairs, frantically attempting to escape the mayhem. Seconds mattered. Dwight and Sharon exited and looked around as they ran toward where the shots originated. They zoomed in on the only building with open and closed windows. They ran inside, following six policemen with guns drawn. They policed the floors one by one. Clearing each room, they knocked on the doors and spoke to anyone who approached them. Dwight found himself on the fifth floor at the beginning of a long hallway. It was a hotel with conventioners just visiting for various lengths of time for different reasons. It was older, and some of the windows hadn't been updated. They still opened and closed. The ones on the north side of the street had a direct line of sight to the area where the press conference was being held. By now, the police had blocked the street. No cars were able to get through the barriers. The priorities of the reporters had shifted from the Mayor's son to the attempt on the Mayor's life.

Dwight felt a familiar lingering aroma. He could smell the air coming down the hall. It was charred, like something had been burned or a firearm had been discharged. The further down the hall he traveled, the stronger the smell became. The sunlight coming into the hall now had a lingering smog. He heard a man's voice coming from Room 19. He slowly crept toward the door and placed his ear as cautiously as he could against the wall. Dwight heard what he understood to be the confirmation of a kill by an assassin. He knocked, and immediately three shots were fired right through the door. Just to the left of the door, Dwight turned, kicked the door in, and saw a man in the room. He was standing dramatically in the middle of the room, holding a cell phone to his head. By the time Dwight could utter any words, the gunman shot at him and missed. Dwight ducked into the bathroom. Dwight looked around the corner to see the gunman taking apart the cell phone as instructed by the voice on the other end of the call. He took the small chip inside the phone and held it to his lips. With a slight hesitation, the gunman put the chip in his mouth and swallowed it. Dwight figured it was the SIM card. There was no way to retrieve the data from the SIM card, which was now deeply embedded in the perpetrator's belly. The gunman seemed satisfied that he had done his duty. All of a sudden, he began to shake nervously. Then, he began to quake violently and fall to the ground. His eyes opened wide and turned dark red. Foam began to well up and spill forth from his lips. Unaware that the SIM card had been laced with a fast-acting poison, he realized that in an instant, the assassin had become the target, a loose end to be disposed of once his mission had been fulfilled. Dwight came out of the bathroom to the sound of the gunman's life succumbing to the poison.

"Man down! Man Down! Fifth floor—Room 19."

Sharon entered the room out of breath. Her gun was drawn and pointing upwards. She saw Dwight lying on the floor through the haze. She saw that the assassin wasn't quite dead. Dwight was speaking to him. Wincing from the pain and fading fast, there wasn't much time for him to say his final words. Dwight asked him who hired him. The assailant could barely muster up the strength to utter the words. "Oh, Bee..., "He whispered as his pupils dilated. He passed before he could utter anything else. Sharon and Dwight paused to try to figure out what that meant. Oh Bee? Maybe the poison had a hallucinogenic effect right before it claimed the life of its victim. Sharon glanced at Dwight —equally confused, with a blank expression. His eyes were wide open and staring at the gunman's face, searching, reaching in his mind for anything relevant to give meaning to the gunman's final words.

Pathologists and other staff had entered the room and started doing tests and gathering evidence as they secured the crime scene. In a matter of minutes, the police had blocked off a 10-block area. No traffic was to get in or out. Policemen and investigators were flooding onto the scene of the building and the hotel across the street. All the guests were interviewed and asked to find alternative accommodations, as the hotel had been quarantined as a crime scene. The hotel became flooded with various other personnel prepared to canvas the area and gather what might serve as clues as to who ordered this attempt on the Mayor's life, and why. The Mayor was transported immediately with a police escort to the Hospital with one gunshot to the chest. There were four shots fired that Dwight could recall. Only one found its way to the Mayor. Now with the son gone and the Mayor shot, it was as important as ever to solve this case.

It would be easy to say it was an "old-school vendetta." Carl Kinsingsworth double-crossed the wrong Mafia Boss, and the boss decides to kill everyone in his family. Maybe it is that simple. They need more clues. So far, nothing they have is conclusive. There's not even enough to invent a scenario. Jerry Mack came storming in with an entourage of reporters and various personnel buzzing around him. Dwight and Sharon met him in the lobby and provided their statements regarding what happened on the fifth floor. Jerry admonished them to complete a report before heading to Boston to canvas Harvard Law School for clues. Exiting the Regal Hotel, they could see the press camped out in front of the building conducting interviews and giving live reports to their affiliate stations. Vans with giant letters painted on the sides indicated the various stations. They managed to make it past the blockade and set up in front of the hotel's huge revolving door. When reporters tried to approach the two detectives for an interview, Dwight and Sharon ducked out and ran to their car. They immediately got in the vehicle and drove off—out of breath and adrenaline pumping. Even without Dwight and Sharon's statements, the press had hold of the story, and by six o'clock, it was on the evening news. Dwight and Sharon arranged to visit David's Alma mater, confident that the investigative team assigned to the assassination attempt was working things out on their end.

# Chapter Seven-Storm in the Dorm

The flight took one and a half hours, and the two wasted no time. While on the plane, they managed to find and contact the Dormitory administrator of David's freshman dorm. Her name was Haley Thurman. She said that David and she knew each other well. She also agreed to an interview. So, that's where Sharon and Dwight headed first. The fair weather made the drive to the campus pleasant; however, to look more 'official,' Dwight and Sharon opted for Dark sunglasses with square frames to shield their eyes from the blinding New England daylight. Once they pulled up to the building, they noticed a fresh-faced girl with her hair pulled back in a ponytail, holding a clipboard cradled in her arms like a child. Haley wore a pair of sunglasses on her head to keep her hair out of her face. She wore a light yellow sweater draped over both shoulders. It looked soft like cashmere or angora. She waved at the car containing our two investigators and signaled them to park in the space she had picked out just for them. They introduced themselves and flashed the customary identification (i.e., badge), and Haley escorted them inside the building to David's freshman dorm room. Casually, they looked around his belongings. Without a warrant, they couldn't thoroughly search the room. So, they visually looked around, hoping to see something that would give them probable cause to ask a judge for a warrant to search.

Sharon thought it was odd that the two beds in the room were both made up, as if the two inhabitants weren't expecting to return for a while. There was a desk with a computer and a printer. There was a shared bookshelf with books on political science, philosophy, and poetry. A few comic books and three cross-country skiing trophies lined the shelves. There was also a picture of Candice Kinsingsworth—his mother posing with his father, Carl.

"That's his parents—Candice and Carl. Very nice people."

"Would it be okay, Miss Thurman, if we asked you a few questions about David?"

"Sure."

"Did David exhibit any unusual behavior in the past four days?"

"He seemed really tense, but I just thought it was just because he was preparing to go back home to see his family, and he was afraid of missing his flight."

"Did he have many friends here at school? People that he hung out with?"

"He had his girlfriend and his best friend, Kyle. He and Kyle went everywhere together. Well, they were best friends after all. His girlfriend lived near where he grew up. She visited occasionally, but usually because they were both catching a flight back to Chicago together. David was going to visit his parents."

"What was the girlfriend's name?"

"Jennifer. He called her Jenny—Jenny Foster. She lives off campus now. You can probably look her up in the student directory."

"What can you tell us about Jenny Foster? How did they meet? How long have they been seeing each other?"

"Well, I don't know much about her or her background. She just started hanging around David one day, and all of a sudden, he starts telling everyone that she is his fiancée. Isn't that odd?"

"Odd because they hadn't known each other very long before they decided to get engaged?"

"Yeah! I mean, make sure he is the one before you commit to a lifetime with this person."

"Thank you, Miss Thurman. What can you tell us about Kyle? Do you know his full name?"

"Yes, Kyle Templeman. Like I said, he and David were inseparable. They met here on Campus. The roommate gods had put them together as freshmen. They quickly hit it off and soon they were seen arriving at school parties together, and going on road trips together. David even took him back to Chicago to meet his parents. His father and David's father knew each other through some business dealings, and when they came here to live on Campus as roommates, it was natural that they would become buds. I think I overheard a conversation about David, his Dad, Kyle, and his dad, and how they were planning a trip to Kyle's family cabin retreat— to do some fishing and hunting somewhere in Maine or Vermont. I'm not sure which."

After a few more questions, they could paint a picture of David's life as a college student. They felt like the next step would be to try to connect with Jennifer Foster, David's fiancée. After some sleuthing, they managed to find out that she lived in a studio apartment near the Campus. She worked at a coffee shop a short walk from her studio. The two approached her as she was leaving for work. She was apprehensive when they approached her. After Dwight and Sharon explained the purpose of their visit, she agreed to meet them after work and discuss David's relationship with her.

She was rather like the girl next door. She had hazel eyes and auburn hair. The kind of "normal" that would appeal to the most discerning of conservative parents. She worked at the coffee shop and volunteered where she met Mrs. Kinsingsworth, at one of the Kinsingsworth's charities. They worked well together and shared their thoughts on politics, religion, and marriage. With Mrs. Kinsingsworth's approval, they were introduced and encouraged to date. Jennifer did not have the advantages that David did. She was a hard-working, pre-law student on a scholarship. David was a political science major and party monster. What impressed her most was his charisma and ability to charm anyone. What impressed him about Haley was that her beauty was equally matched by her focus and determination. This drive and inner fire caused David to befriend and open his heart to her. He had never felt this way about a woman before Haley, which also impressed him about her. They dated for about four months, and David proposed. She had just begun making plans for the wedding when the news came about David's disappearance and the attempt on Mayor Kinsingsworth's life. She planned to fly to Chicago to visit Mrs. Kinsingsworth during her great sorrow.

Sharon felt that something wasn't right. This feeling came from her as a woman rather than a hard-nosed detective. She didn't want to disappoint Dwight by exposing her femininity, but she couldn't help feeling that Miss Foster was hiding something. At the very least, she was withholding some important information about David. Detectives are trained to spot inconsistencies in behavior and contradictions in an eyewitness account during an investigation. Precisely what it was, they couldn't get her to say it. Whatever it was, she concealed it with the grace of a socialite. What was she hiding that she would risk charges to keep her secret safe?

Sharon had the FBI do a background check on Jennifer and Kyle. Jennifer was born and raised in Massachusetts. Her parents were Donald and Francine Foster. She had a pretty uneventful childhood. Her family worked hard and saved everything they could to afford to send Jennifer to Harvard. No record of any criminal activity, not even a misdemeanor. She was Miss Massachusetts 2001. She didn't belong to any social groups or campus organizations. She didn't have too many friends to speak of. Her life was full. Aside from her secular job, school, and her charity work for the Kinsingsworths, she enjoyed going to yoga class and Pilates. Dwight thought it was odd that when Jennifer received the news about David's disappearance, she made no immediate arrangements to be with the family. It was the attempt on the Mayor's life that moved her enough to fly to Chicago to be with them. Indeed, during the interview, her concern seemed underwhelming. For a newly engaged fiancée to a prominent political family, such as the Kinsingsworths, she seemed distant from them as if she wasn't welcomed or accepted by them. No expressions of worry or signs of stress. Just a woman, tired from a long day of working on her feet in a coffee shop. Most young women would be radiant at the thought of being considered, in America, the equivalent of a princess engaged to a prince.

Other oddities kept creeping into Dwight's mind. Why was Mrs. Kinsingsworth so insistent that her son marry while still in Law School? Celebrating an engagement of only four months seemed out of character for such staunch conservatives as they were. She would have surely gotten some side-eyes from her peers because of such a short-lived courtship period. Dwight felt that Jennifer's parents should have been a little more protective of their daughter, requiring her to wait until she got to know her fiancée a little better before deciding to spend the rest of her life with him. It just felt like the more questions of theirs that she answered, the more questions they should have asked. They weren't getting the whole story and will probably revisit Miss Foster soon. The focus shifted to the one common denominator in both of the girls' stories. Immediately, Dwight and Sharon started trying to locate Kyle Templeman. The student directory said that Kyle did not live far from the campus. FBI research supported the claims that Kyle's father, Frank Jacob Templeman, and David's father, Carl Kinsingsworth, were indeed friends. While David was a political science major, Kyle was getting a Bachelor of Science degree in Sports Management. As a freshman, he was a member of the Harvard Wrestling team. Indeed, Kyle was David's roommate and best friend. They were seen together in both Boston and Chicago. The FBI sent over a current photo of Kyle. He was tall (6 ft. 2"), 210 lbs of blond-haired, blue-eyed muscle. Classic All-American looks and athleticism, he was an alpha male, an extrovert, and charismatic. His schedule consisted of morning workouts, classes, wrestling practice, and homework —sometimes in the dorm or the library.

With a busy schedule, Dwight wondered how any of them found time to attend events and parties, fly to Chicago on weekends, and have affairs with different people. Only one person would be able to shed some light on the subject—Kyle Templeman, the subject himself. Sharon imagined a tiny room and the two gentlemen walking in and introducing themselves to each other. They didn't know each other or how they would live together. They didn't know how the next few years would play out for either of them. In her mind, David was at the computer, computing. Then, randomly, the door swings open and a strapping young blond guy stands in the doorway holding two suitcases. One under his armpit and one in his left hand. With a ball in the other hand and effortlessness, he kicked the door open to David's face, staring back at him in surprise. David turns and returns to the screen, beginning to type again. David is frozen, and Kyle doesn't move. Kyle just stares at David and starts sizing him up (not as tall, probably a nerd, has a girlfriend, and has Daddy's money).

David finishes typing his paragraph, turns around, and immediately notices Kyle's size and stature. David looks him up and down. Kyle doesn't budge, and David notices that Kyle is holding two large suitcases at the same time. Kyle waits for David's reaction, but David just remains stoic. Minutes pass, and Kyle is stalwart and unyielding. Impressed by this behavior, David's computer screen times out and concedes to the young man standing in the doorway. He invites Mr. Templman to come in and put his things away. With no cramps or fatigue, Kyle walks in and puts his luggage on the ground in front of the bed by the door. "You play ball?" Those magical first words were their first interaction. Days go by. The two men become accustomed to being around each other. David helps Kyle with his homework while Kyle is at wrestling practice. Many times, Kyle would return to the dorm, sweating and exhausted. He would peel off his clothes, shower, finish his homework, and sleep—rinse and repeat.

Many of David's evenings were spent doing research in the library. The two barely spoke. David's silence was perceived as shyness, whereas Kyle, with his busy life, didn't have time for idle chit-chat. They had nothing in common. However, continuing this way would make for a long first semester. Kyle, the alpha male, decided to take matters into his own hands and "shake things up a little." He randomly invites David to a party for the wrestling team. David, also not a fan of the mundane, looks at the opportunity to start networking with the other students on campus. Kyle could be his ticket to conquering his shyness. He could be more extroverted, and Kyle could be the one to bring David out of his shell. The party was a big success. It was more than a party. The two would become social adventurers together, attending more parties and events that took them to various destinations. Some of the places they visited were secret, exotic, and sometimes forbidden. Together, they met interesting people and experienced many of the joys that this life has to offer. They made trips to Vegas, Chicago, New York, Los Angeles, among others.

The young bachelors even experienced things that only men of their caliber would be privileged to see. Things that could be considered "taboo" or of a "Darker Nature." Through their network of contacts, the parties became increasingly exclusive. The experiences became more and more "risky." While David reveled in his newfound liberation from monotony, Kyle began to show his disdain for some things that he had seen. One night, they went to a private party on a yacht in Miami and had drinks with some buddies they had met on the party circuit. They mentioned a beautiful nightclub tucked away in an alley in downtown Chicago. They texted the information to David. He was so excited that Kyle and he were going on another adventure together, to the world's most beautiful Drag Club in Chicago, called "The Lido." Kyle said he no longer wanted to be part of the scene. Through his forged kinship and charismatic nature, David persuaded his wrestler buddy to go one last time. He promised Kyle that this would be the last one before they finished school, got their degrees, settled down, archived this chapter under the heading: "The Glory Days," and prepared to enter the next phase of their lives.

Our detective duo pulled up to a luxury apartment complex and took the elevator to 14 B. It was at the end of the hall. Walking up to the apartment, they could hear the faint noise of a carpet steamer operating in one of the bedrooms. Dwight unplugged the cord from the wall, which immediately turned it off. An elderly woman entered the living area and jumped at the sight of Dwight and Sharon standing there, flashing identification. She was a relative of Kyle's. Her name was Angelina Kinney. She said that Kyle had moved out of the apartment, and she had been cleaning it up for him. When asked why he picked up and left so suddenly, she said she didn't know. She just received a text and a cash transfer of $250.00, asking Angelina if she could get his deposit back. She didn't have the money, but said she would. When asked where he may have gone, Miss Kinney said that he probably headed to Chicago to hang out with his buddy from college, David something. She also said they must hurry to catch him if they wanted to speak to him, because his flight leaves in 35 minutes. The two thanked her for the information and for taking time out of her task to answer their questions.

With no time to hesitate, they headed straight for the airport. Traffic was heavy, but they arrived on time. Dwight bolted from the car, disturbing traffic and crossing to the Large sliding glass doors of the main entrance. He was risking his life to possibly catch Kyle before he could board his flight to Chicago. It was difficult maneuvering through the crowd and navigating the long concourse to reach the gate where Kyle was boarding the plane. Jumping over escalators and mowing down innocent bystanders couldn't help Dwight get to the gate any faster. As he ran to the boarding desk, he watched the airplane's door close and lock, and watched the plane pull away from the gate, and 'taxi' down the runway. It was too late to try to delay the flight for official business. There was no time to obtain a warrant to remove him from the plane anyway. Sharon soon caught up with Dwight, and she could already see the look of defeat on Dwight's face."So, what's next?"

"Book us two flights to Chicago and put out an A.P.B. on Kyle Templeman. Give them the Airline and flight number. Tell them to be ready to take him in for questioning, and do it quickly before he has a chance to ' Lawyer up'."

"Let's go, Dwight! We're going home."

# Chapter Eight-A Tale of Two Tables

They pulled up to the precinct headquarters and were immediately summoned to Jerry Mack's office for a brief meeting. Jerry Mack had the DNA results from the body that was dumped at the pier. It's almost supernatural—the instincts and hunches that Dwight has. After years of being a detective, his experience enabled him to hone his instincts to a science. The tests revealed that the body on the pier was none other than the missing mayor's son, David Kinsingsworth.

"Better head on down to the morgue, the mother is on her way to positively identify both bodies." Standing in a sallow green room is the tiny frame of a woman in grief. She is sobbing and clinging to a white handkerchief. She is waiting to be allowed into the adjoining room, where two tables have been set up, each with a body shrouded in white plastic. A group of men surrounds the tables. They are dressed in green scrubs with white hats and masks. One of the men had a light on his forehead and a pair of glasses. They all wore gloves. Before meeting Mrs. Kinsingsworth, the head coroner quickly oriented the staff on some pointers about professional etiquette when meeting the victim's families. Everyone nods in agreement and starts to remove their gloves. As the green clothing comes off, it is revealed that the officials standing with the head coroner were the commissioner and our two detectives, Sharon and Dwight. All were present to assist Mrs. Kinsingsworth in identifying the deceased. All attention was given to the mother as they opened the door and ushered her into the room. No words were spoken. They all knew why she was there and didn't want this experience to add to her already unbearable feelings of guilt, loss, and grief.

Solemnly, she enters the room and saunters to the two tables. Strategically placed for maximum convenience, near the door, in the center of the room, she could exit the area quickly, if needed. They were to be the main focus of the next ten minutes. Mrs. Kinsingsworth stood between them. At what she thought was the head of the two tables. The coroner pulled back the first shroud, revealing the pale, sleeping face of the mayor. The weight of the fact that her husband was assassinated in cold blood was too much, and she cried out in pain. She grabbed her abdomen and hunched over to let out a cry that only a woman with years of love and devotion could have cried. The group present couldn't help but feel that they were seeing her die a little in that moment as well. They quickly escorted her back to the viewing room, where she could calm down and collect herself to repeat the procedure for her son. It took what seemed like hours before she could re-enter the room. She realized that she needed to keep it together and get through this next one, so when the coroner pulled back the plastic for the second body, she stood tall but could not stop the tears from streaming down her face. She nodded her head to let the record show that the two bodies were indeed her husband and son. By then, two close friends arrived, waiting for her to finish. They were going to take her home and let her rest before she began the task of arranging their final resting places and funeral proceedings. There was so much to do. "Dwight, they found Templeman."

"He is being held at the precinct."

"Let's get down there. I would like to question Mr. Templeman myself."

Kyle was apprehended as he was exiting the plane. They brought him in for questioning. Now sitting in the interrogation room, He wasn't as worried about why they brought him in as much as the fact that his best friend and former lover vanished from Kyle's life. The darkened room, the blood, kept him from realizing that he was about to be accused of murder in the first degree. He also did not remember having one phone call as part of 'due process.' His Lawyer was just a few cell phone taps away. Kyle kept telling himself that he did what he had to do. His mind wanders back to his life with David and Harvard. He remembers when they met. The romantic times they shared and how they tried so hard to keep it a secret from everyone they knew. Yes, what seemed like the perfect pairing of friend and lover was nothing more than the act of satisfying an aching curiosity, fueled by youth and hormonal urges. A hard lesson for anyone to learn is that a relationship is the participation of two independent beings bound by the heart. The problem is that people change. Circumstances change. Life changes, and the person you entered into this bond with may enjoy the relationship, even find it all-encompassing and fulfilling. Sometimes they don't. Their feelings change often, and suddenly, the person with whom you shared your life and formed a deep connection becomes a stranger. It's alright to ignore the first few instances when this happens.

However, when the realization that they have changed starts to settle in, the passion turns to resentment and anger. No matter the measures taken to counteract the inevitable, eventually, you realize that the time you have enjoyed with them will end, even if they promise otherwise. The door is closing. It's obvious. Nothing or no one can stop it. It's time to prepare for the breakup and move forward. Kyle was not ready for the morning when he woke and saw David beside him. David was welling up with a sadness that Kyle could feel. He told Kyle that he wanted them to "just be friends." Kyle asked him to clarify the situation. Then he asked for an explanation. David was terrible at verbalizing what he was feeling. Perhaps it was because David didn't know how to express to his best friend that he didn't share the same depth of feeling for Kyle as Kyle had for him. David's decision to end things with Kyle felt wrong. However, not as wrong as being untruthful with Kyle. So,

David was as honest with Kyle as he could be. He owed him that. Kyle couldn't conceal his broken heart. He got up and went to the gym. He could ignore his hurt feelings in a rigorous workout. He felt that he could manage his toxic, negative emotions with sweat equity. When he got home, David had packed up and moved out of the dorm. David was heading back to Chicago. Kyle felt the void of David's absence in the room. It was an unbearable silence. It surprised him that outside he was tough as steel, but on the inside, he still had a soft spot for his first love. Staying in the little room held no purpose for him any longer, so Kyle began gathering his things and moved to an apartment just off campus. The unresolved emotions ate away at him until he decided to put his feelings aside and do something proactive.

Sharon pulled up the FBI report on Kyle Christopher Templeman. He was attending Harvard on an athletic scholarship. Aside from his major, he was a member of an organization he called "Other Brother." He did a lot of charitable work with children in the Boston area. Reading the list of accomplishments, she noticed that he is a runner. He ran in the Boston Marathon. Although he did not complete the marathon, he thoroughly enjoyed the experience and plans to run it again. He was single, except for his time with David, and didn't date anyone on or off campus. He held several jobs. His most notable one was a brief time on a farm. It was a good fit for him. He thought that he looked the part. He saw it as an opportunity to connect with nature. He enjoyed it so much that he convinced his dad to purchase a small cabin by a lake where he enjoys hunting and fishing on the weekends.

Eyewitnesses place him in Chicago and Miami with David, bringing us to now. Kyle was alone in the interrogation room. Behind him was a one-way mirror. Behind that stood Dwight, Sharon, and Jerry Mack. Dwight stared at Kyle in silence. Sharon walked in with the FBI report and handed it to Dwight. He recognized what it was and started thumbing through it. Dwight read a couple of entries and closed the file. "What is it, Dwight?"

"They are searching Jimmy Rantor's apartment. They found blood on the bed and floor. It is now considered a crime scene. Do you want to come with me and check it out?"

"Sure, I'll meet you downstairs," Sharon said. She headed to the elevator when her friend, Lillie, stopped her to say "HI." They knew each other back in college. When Sharon saw her, she hugged Lilly and started talking about The Spring break they had in Cabo. They could have talked all afternoon, but Sharon had to meet Dwight to go to Jimmy's Apartment. That's when Lillie mentioned that she was working on the same case in the forensics lab. In particular, she was in the process of decoding the encrypted files from "Other Brother Website." She said they should solve it in the next day or two. Sharon was ecstatic and gave Lillie her phone number to call so they could get lunch sometime and to keep her posted on the progress with the website. One last hug, and Sharon got on the elevator to the first floor.

As they arrived on the scene, they noticed it was within walking distance of Pier 14. The apartment was located above a storefront in a tourist-friendly area of Chicago, near the water. It was a small loft with high ceilings and windows throughout. It was quaint, featuring classic New England architecture, ample natural light, and tasteful decoration. It consisted of four rooms. The front entrance opened up into the living room from the hallway. The only way to access the apartment door was by climbing a flight of stairs and taking the landing to the very end. A single window at the top of the stairs was illuminated. There were two lights as well. One of them was burned out. The landing was made of wood. It creaked when you walked on it. The walls were brick and cinder block. They were recently painted beige and dark red. The windows and the rail were a dark green. It had a charming waterfront feel. The windows were oversized, with sheer white curtains that filtered out the light to create a feeling of relaxation and sanctuary. The living room had a small sofa, a coffee table, and a television. A couple of paintings were on the wall, and a small lamp sat on a table beside the couch. A little cactus plant adorned it. Nothing had been touched. The building had been "taped off" with "Caution" tape. Forensics was wrapping up, gathering all the evidence they needed to run DNA tests.

To the right was a galley kitchen with a single countertop and a few cabinets overhead and under the counter. A white stove and refrigerator needed to be updated. A small table and two chairs were set up in the nook, bistro style. Everything in the kitchen was white except the walls. They were a golden yellow color with painted white trim and moulding. Everything was put away. All of the counters were wiped clean and dried. The refrigerator was empty except for a partially eaten piece of cheese cake with a tiny pink and white striped candle poking out of it. The candle was not lit, but the cake had several bites taken out of it. Then there was the bedroom and master bathroom. It was on the other side of the apartment. To access the bedroom from the kitchen, the living room's laminate floor had to be traversed, with a large area rug providing a path to the bedroom doorway. The bedroom had two long, narrow windows in the corner, overlooking the street. The bed was positioned in the middle of the room against the longest wall. It did not have a headboard or frame. It was just a box spring and mattress on the floor. It was stained in shades of pink and red with yellow and brown marbling. The stain continued to the floor on the side away from the door. There was some splattering on the wall, but not directional and widespread as if from a gunshot, which led Dwight to believe that there was not much of a struggle. The murder weapon may not have been a gun. Additionally, the bed was stained in a curved outline similar to that of an adult human being. However, the bed was just stained. There were no holes or slices in it. Indicating that the weapon of choice was short to medium length, five to nine inches. Next to the bed was a nightstand with a drawer. The single top drawer was empty. The cabinet underneath the nightstand was open and empty. A phone charger was beside the bed, but no phone was found anywhere.

"Ask forensics if they recovered a phone anywhere in the apartment."

"I'm on it."

In the doorway, on the floor in front of the door, there were crumbs of green leaves and a handful of dried and shrunken pink rose petals—the remnants of a bouquet of pink roses wrapped in green tissue paper. The paper was printed with the words "Nickel Bud's Flower Shoppe." Dwight made a few inquiries and discovered that Nickel Bud's Flower Shoppe was at the end of the block. They did, in fact, carry pink roses. The last bouquet was purchased five days ago. The purchaser paid cash and didn't give his name. The description that was given matched Kyle's size and build. The security footage showed a large figure with broad shoulders busting through the door holding the bouquet in his hands. Upon examining the doorway to the apartment, Dwight could see that the door had been damaged, but there were a few indents outside of the main door. Dwight took his hand and contorted it into different shapes. The only shape that seemed to look like it was capable of making dents in a door like that would have to be a fist pounding on the door so hard that it would do this kind of damage to a heavy metal door. The wood was torn from the door jam, but only the chain and the first of the three locks were locked. The rest were left unlocked. Dwight recalled that Kyle's knuckles on his left hand were of color. They were purple-ish pink, unlike the pale skin of his other hand. It was inconclusive, but the bruising could have been caused by the pounding of a betrayed suitor. All of these details were just observations that Dwight filed away in his mind to pull up later, when they became relevant. This was a technique he had practiced since becoming a detective. It has served him well when trying to put together scenarios.

"If you are going to question Kyle, you'd better get back to the precinct. He's asked for his lawyer to be present during the questioning." Dwight and Sharon headed back to headquarters. When Dwight and Sharon arrived to question the suspect, his lawyer had already sent him home. The lawyer said that his client was being unlawfully detained and, unless they were going to formally arrest him, he was free to go. So, Dwight and Sharon decided to research the organization that Kyle allegedly belonged to, Other Brother, and wait for the DNA results. Two Days later, the results revealed that the DNA of the blood found at the apartment did not match Kyle's at all. In fact, the evidence gathered at the scene alluded to the fact that there were only two people in the apartment at the time of the murder. Neither one of them was Kyle Templeman. Kyle could have been the tall figure on the security camera footage breaking in the door, though it is unlikely that he committed the murder. Dwight still thought that Kyle had some light to shed on his buddy's untimely death, even if he isn't a suspect. After all, Mr. Sassman saw them together at the Lido. Kyle was the wingman for his buddy and Miss Davis.

"So, if Kyle was at the crime scene and did not commit the murder, what was he doing there?"

"Well, He and David started frequenting the Lido, met Casandra Davis, and soon became the three Musketeers. He was David's wingman to keep David's affair with Miss Davis out of the public eye. So, what if he was more than just a wing man?"

"The only way to substantiate a love triangle between Casandra Davis, Kyle Templeman, and David Kinsingsworth is to get Kyle to admit that he was involved. It still doesn't reveal who murdered her and David, how David arrived at Pier 14, and why."

"I wish we knew where Kyle disappeared to."

"That's easy. The FBI report says that Kyle persuaded his father to purchase a plot of lake property and build a Cabin there. What better place to get away and clear your head?"

"You're right! It's secluded. Anyone caught on the premises would be trespassing. The police would need a search warrant to even get near it."

"We need to find out where it is and meet Kyle there. He will be comfortable giving a statement in his own familiar surroundings. "Just then, the speaker announced that Dwight needed to pick up a call from Jerry Mack.

Kyle was identified by one of the receptionists at Mercy Regional Hospital, who went to the front desk and spoke with someone there. Immediately, instructions were given to detain him, and our two detectives were on their way. It was a 10-minute drive, weather permitting. Dwight broke every posted speed limit to get to the hospital before Kyle left. Why was he there? The Mayor was taken there for his autopsy. Perhaps Kyle believed the Mayor was still alive and wanted to complete the task that the other hitman had failed to accomplish. That would be a somewhat risky move, but Kyle was a suspect in David's murder anyway. He could've thought he had nothing to lose.

Dwight arrived at the hospital and spoke with the front desk receptionist. She gave them the room number where Kyle was headed. When the detectives inquired as to why he was there, she said he was there to visit someone he brought in approximately a week ago. Just then, a tall blond figure walked past them and started to head for the door. The receptionist gestured toward him to wait and signaled the two detectives that it was him. They asked to talk to him. Just then, as Dwight started to walk toward him, Kyle bolted for the door. It was a long hallway to traverse before he could get to the glowing revolving doors of the hospital and outside, where his chance of a "get away" would be easier to achieve. He started running. He had just taken his first few strides, and a patient on a gurney came out of the elevator and slammed into him. Then Dwight immediately sprang into action, realizing that a chase was underfoot. He took off after Kyle. As Dwight began to chase Kyle down the long hallway, he saw Kyle try to hurdle the gurney and miss. His foot caught the edge of the thin, narrow mattress as he was leaping over it. He plummeted to the ground along with the gurney, the patient, and the orderly who was pushing him, and the intravenous tube taped to the patient's arm, which was rolling along with them out of the elevator. Kyle got up undaunted by the delay and started again.

Dwight had caught up to the gurney and yelled at the bystanders to move out of the way. People gasped as they proceeded to move out of the way of the chase as quickly as they possibly could. Kyle was escaping, and no one was getting in his way. He plowed into a woman waiting to see the doctor, sitting in a chair against the wall. In one giant leap, Kyle hopped onto the arm of the chair and walked or hopped on the arms of all the chairs that lined the walls. His arms were raised and stretched out for balance. Kyle made his way across the waiting patients, looking up at him and frightened at the spectacle of Kyle's daredevil antics. They feared that he would break their chairs and fall. He was careful to avoid anyone with a horrified expression. Some people held up their hands to help him balance so they wouldn't be directly underneath him and possibly feel the solid frame of a college wrestler come bearing down on them as he broke the Scandinavian design, minimalist, ideal chairs. He tore the art piece hanging above them off the wall. As it fell to the ground behind them, he voiced a low grunt in surprise and apologized to the people sitting in the chairs. At the same time, the other people in the room began screaming and running for their lives. They did not want to be a victim of an adrenaline-fueled chase. Crowds of people poured out of the doorway and into the parking lot, spilling onto the street like a stampeding herd of animals. They were screaming in fright and waving their arms to move as quickly as possible to reach their vehicles and escape the chaos. Kyle was picking up speed when a man in green scrubs entered his path and held his hands up in command. Dwight slowed down to allow the doctor to pass. Kyle, however, effortlessly mowed him down. It was enough for Dwight to catch up to him, dive onto Kyle's foot, and hold on for dear life. Kyle did not know how tall and strong Dwight was. Dwight didn't know if he was strong enough to best our wrestling champion. Kyle saw the door, only a few feet away. Then Dwight tackles him, and he goes down. He went down hard. Without a warning, he was taken down to the ground, and this time he had a big strapping police detective holding him down. Unfortunately for Dwight, he was now in Kyle's comfort zone. Kyle's strongest wrestling position in college was on the ground. He rolled over and quickly turned the tide on Dwight. Sharon ran up to the scene. Now that the hospital was empty, the police had the place sectioned off so no one could get in or out. Dwight punched Kyle in the face. Kyle tightened his chokehold. There was so much rolling around and confusion that Sharon could not get a clear shot. Her firearm was drawn. However, she didn't want to risk taking out her partner while also trying to rescue him.

"Listen, man... I will let you go if you hear me out."

"No Chance, Kyle. You're under arrest for the murder of David Kinsingsworth and Casandra Davis A.K.A. Jimmy Ranter." "Look! I'm not a murderer."

"I've got an eye on him, Dwight, move. Let go of him, Kyle, or I'll shoot!"

"Not until I have your word! Hear me out." He loosened his grip. Dwight lay limp on the ground, breathing heavily. Kyle raised both hands in surrender. Sharon told him to kneel on the ground with both hands behind his back. She cuffed him and raised him to his feet.

"You promised you would hear me out!"

"No. I promised I wouldn't shoot you. Well, you're still alive." Sharon mused as she walked him to the squad car and watched him squeeze into the back seat. Dwight walked out with his hands massaging his neck and forehead. "Man! That Kid's gotta grip!"

"You should have let me shoot him."

"Yeah, but you probably would have shot me instead."

"Hey! I aced my target shooting test at the academy."

"It would have been an accident; I'll give you that. Anyway, thanks for not taking the shot!"

"What do you think he's going to say?" Dwight didn't answer.

He made a gesture towards the car. Sharon got in. Dwight's plan is to let Kyle say what he wanted to say and be done. No predictions, no judgements. They made their way back to the precinct. Kyle was back in the interrogation room. Only now he was in handcuffs. The police department didn't want to take any chances that Kyle might get away. Dwight and Sharon stood in the adjacent room, looking through the one-way mirror. They could only hear the muffled whining of Kyle asking to tell someone his story. Dwight wondered if he might indeed be looking at the face of the killer of the Mayor's son. There was no solid evidence either way. If Dwight feels a reasonable doubt, the jury might feel the same.

The pleading eventually stopped. Kyle just sat in silence. Still in cuffs, he hung his head down and drifted in his mind to Jimmy. He wonders if Jimmy had ever sat in a room like this, and in handcuffs like this. Kyle had never been arrested before. He thinks back to the conversation he had with David in the dorm room about his confession, and he was going to break it off with Casandra. Kyle knew that she would not take the news well. He wanted to know how David could be so cold-hearted. That's when David said that once he gave up the 'party life' for a life of sobriety and dependability, he would eventually like to settle down and pursue a life in politics, like his father Carl, possibly with a wife and kids too. Then, almost simultaneously, he switched memories to his conversation with Casandra Davis. He started sobbing, and tears began to stream down his face.

Kyle went to see Casandra at her apartment. She was painting her toes just after getting out of the shower. She threw her robe on to let Kyle in the door. But he had a key and opened it himself. He said that he had to talk to her about something important. However, before he could get the words out, she announced bluntly that she was breaking up with him. Frozen and speechless, Kyle turned in defeat and headed out into the hall, but his curiosity made him swallow his pride, turn around, and ask why. Casandra was honest and straightforward so that nothing could be misconstrued. She was in love with David, and she was going to marry him. Kyle was so devastated that he didn't tell her that David had plans to end his relationship with her. Kyle failed to say that David didn't have the same feelings for her that she did for him. Kyle also didn't tell her he was in love with her. No, he just left the apartment, got into his car, and left. Kyle reflected on all the passion he and Casandra shared—their bodies, their minds. They would have deep emotional conversations in the middle of the night.

He recalls the night he met her for the first time. It was during Pride month. A warm day in June. There was a pride party in the parking lot of the Lido. Many people were angry. The place where they used to park their vehicles was now blocked off and turned into an outdoor nightclub and performance venue. Kyle and David had to walk five blocks to get to the club. However, the energy was amazing once the party got into full swing. It was the celebration of a lifetime for these two young men. Casandra came out and performed her first set. The two guys were instantly mesmerized by her beauty and glamour. "Smoke and Mirrors is all it is," she would say. Her gesture as she spoke was a wave of the hands as if to perform an imaginary feat of magic. She was captivating, and David and Kyle wanted more. She told the crowd to close their eyes and manifest rain to cool things off. They obeyed. And just as she started the music, all kidding aside, it began to rain. Undaunted by the idea of her makeup ruining in the rain, she, as any professional would, went out on the slippery, wet stage and performed anyway. However, she changed her number to: "You'll never be alone – Barbara Streisand." The crowd loved it so much that they came onto the parking lot in the rain and joined her. She was getting soaked. So, Kyle and David took off their shirts, and two strangers held the garment over her head and angled it so that rain would run off behind her. David tucked his shirt into the back of his shorts. These two, half-naked men, garnered a lot of admiration from the onlookers.

The party raged and the three danced all night in the rain. After the show, they went to Casandra's apartment, dried off, and passed out until the next morning. Kyle woke up and saw David in Miss Davis' bed while Kyle had passed out on the couch. The conversation essentially boiled down to a decision that whatever happens at the Lido, stays at the Lido—typical. For that whole semester, David and Kyle would drive to the Lido to watch the show. David and Casandra would return to her apartment while

Kyle would drive David's white Porsche back to the dorm, with the past weekend being the only exception. Occasionally, Casandra would drive to Harvard to visit David and Kyle, too. That's when she started to get deeply attached to Kyle. He felt the same about her. The two began to realize that there was something there, an attraction. This eventually led to Casandra and Kyle seeing each other at the dorm when David was at the Library studying or writing a term paper. Kyle remembers the nights of ecstasy as if they were yesterday. Again, he starts sobbing."What's going on with this guy?" Sharon asked herself. "Something tells me we are about to find out!"

# Chapter Nine-The Enemy of Mine Enemy

Dwight saw that the sobbing was over. Kyle looked drawn. He was exhausted and tired. His once tensed-up frame was now a limp body slumped in defeat. A bead of sweat gently fell from his brow to the table. He wiped it off the table with his hand. It seemed like an eternity. Thoughts of his attorney started to creep into his mind. It would be simple to request his attorney once more and be free. He could find a better time to ditch the officers and return to the hospital. Then, he heard the door knob slowly turn. It was Dwight entering the room. "Came for round two..." Dwight smirked at the irony because Kyle was still in handcuffs. Dwight slowly walked around him. Didn't speak a word to him. Just stared at him. This made Kyle uneasy. Like a wolf pacing back and forth before his next meal, Dwight made no sudden moves.

"No lawyer?"

"No," Kyle muttered. The quiet, somber response was indicative of his defeat.

Dwight came around the table and eyed the chair across from Kyle. Same exact chair—just on the opposite side. He circles back the other way and slowly walks to Kyle's back. Kyle's heightened awareness kept him attuned to the noises behind him. There was a rattling of change in Dwight's pocket. The confusion made Kyle uneasy and nervous. He was mentally preparing himself for anything that might come. Then, without a warning, he felt the cuffs unlock and come off his wrists.

"I might be wrong, but I don't feel you are here for a rematch."

"Look, I wasn't trying to hurt you or anyone. I just wanted to get you to back off and let me speak to you."

"Well, that's a helluva way to get my attention. It also worked. Here we are. Just you and me."

Dwight kept pace as he made his way to the other side of the table. He kept one eye on the chair and one eye on Kyle. Here he was, face to face, with a murder suspect. Dwight was also nervous, but trained himself to control his emotions. The goal is to uncover the truth and administer justice accordingly. He has played verbal chess countless times before, against all manner of malevolent scum. Here is a kid who has everything going for him, risking it all to kill his best friend? It doesn't make sense.

Jealousy? David had more money than Kyle. David was better connected than Kyle. Dwight has seen homeless people kill each other over a piece of sidewalk they claimed was their territory. So, a similar scenario wouldn't have been that much of a stretch. Drugs? Maybe he was under the influence and murdered them while on a narcotics binge of some sort? Kyle was an athlete. He was all about clean and healthy living. So he wouldn't let the party take over control of his faculties. The only way to understand why he did it is to hear it from Kyle's lips. So, Dwight threw one leg over the empty chair, planted himself across from Kyle, and put both elbows on the table, staring right into Kyle's eyes. There was a period of silence. Who was going to speak first?

"Why'd you do it?"

"Do what? Go to the Hospital? I was visiting a sick friend!"

"C'MON KYLE!! WE KNOW YOU KILLED DAVID!!"

"WHY WOULD I KILL MY BEST FRIEND? ...I loved David. We went everywhere! I was his wingman! I covered for him when he started seeing Jimmy...Sorry—Casandra. He was like the brother I never had. No, I am here to make a deal. I tell you what is really going on and..."

"And what! We let you go free?"

"No! You provide me with police protection!"

"What do you mean? Why in the hell would you need police protection?"

"Because of what I am about to tell you..."

"THAT'S BULLSHIT KYLE! We have you on surveillance cameras! You were seen entering Casandra's apartment on the night that she and David were killed. If you fast forward the footage, it also shows you leaving the crime scene. Forensics looked at your phone records, and you were 'pinged' at the exact location of the murder and Pier 14 at 3:30 am Sunday morning.

"ARE YOU GONNA KEEP BLABBERIN' OR ARE YOU GONNA HEAR ME OUT? SHUT UP FOR JUST A SECOND! WILL YA'?"

"Fine," Dwight complied.

"It was Antonio who killed David."

"THIS IS JUST GETTING CRAZIER! YOU BETTER GET YOUR LAWYER NOW, BECAUSE YOU ARE GOING AWAY FOR A VERY LONG TIME."

"I KNOW IT SOUNDS CRAZY! IT IS CRAZY!" Kyle became very agitated at the sight of some plainclothes police officers roaming the hallways just outside. One was walking by, talking on a cell phone. Two more walked past the door and simultaneously looked in to see Kyle and Dwight sitting at the table in the small room. Kyle leans forward and starts to whisper.

"You have no idea how big this is."

"There is no need to whisper, Kyle." Kyle motions toward the door through which Dwight had come earlier.

"Antonio was hired to kill David and Casandra. They have infiltrated every aspect of government, on every level. You would never know. Antonio is known in my circle as the 'Black Widow's Ghost.'"

"You're talking in riddles! Who are they?"

"It's true! If you want to take someone out, all you have to do is make a call, transfer the funds, and it's as good as done."

"Okay! Let's just say for one freakin' second that this is true; which it's not. It seems like bullshit to me."

"I am telling you it's not."

"Fine. Then, why hasn't the FBI heard of Antonio—the 'Black Widow's Ghost'?"

"Are you dense? He's a ghost! No one knows who he is! No one has ever seen him! And if you have, then you're dead! YOU GOTTA BELIEVE ME!! I AM NOT MAKING THIS UP!"

"I'm gonna need a second to process what I just heard," Dwight says, getting up from the table and leaving. "Don't move. If you for once blink in the direction of that door, I will shoot you myself."

Dwight walked out of the door to the interrogation room and immediately into the observation room where Sharon and Jerry Mack had been listening the whole time. Dwight put one hand on his hip and hung his head in embarrassment. He didn't even know where to begin discussing what he had heard Kyle say. Could there be a bigger picture going on here? We are, after all, not talking about petty criminals. We are talking about high-profile individuals. Privileged youth with money, power, and connections. "What do you guys think? Do you think he is going for 'temporary insanity'?"

"Could just be the desperation of someone facing life in prison. A lie fabricated to keep himself from going to jail."

"He's had every opportunity to play the lawyer card and didn't. He is asking for police protection because he is afraid of 'Other Brother' coming after him for giving us information on this 'Black Widow's Ghost' character."

"While the FBI didn't have any information on the 'Black Widow's Ghost', they did have information on Other Brother." Jerry Mack opened a dossier from the Federal Bureau of Investigation. Thumbing through some papers, he came across a page that explained who Other Brother was, "It says in order to join Other Brother, you must be sworn to secrecy. They perform ritualistic ceremonies similar to hazing, which allows new members to demonstrate their commitment and loyalty to the brotherhood. Some of the members get tattooed with the acronym O.B. On some obscure part of the body."

"Did David's autopsy say whether he had any tattoos, birthmarks, or odd scarring on any part of his body?"

"No marks. Not at all."

"Kyle has one. A scar behind his ear. I noticed it while walking around him right before I sat down to question him. It was two initials—a capital "O" period and a capital "B" period. (O.B.)"

"He looks very nervous right now."

"He was looking at the two officers pacing back and forth in front of the door. One was on his cell phone."

"That's an easy fix. We'll just clear the hallway."

"I'm gonna go back in there and see if there is anything that Kyle can tell us about the night of the murder that can shed some light on the evidence." Dwight exited and re-entered Kyle's room. He resumed sitting across from the suspect, folded his arms, and looked at Kyle. "We looked at the footage again. You were the only one seen on camera entering and exiting Jimmy's apartment. Admittedly, the camera image is dark and grainy. We know it was raining that night. So, I am going to have to get a statement from you about what happened?"

"I should get a lawyer. I thought you were going to be fair. I see that it is not possible for you."

"You are a suspect for murder! First Degree! Forgive me if I am not going to 'jump on your cock- a- mi- mi conspiracy theory Bullshit story', Kyle."

"You don't get it! I am risking my life by allowing myself to get caught. I belong to an organization called Other Brother. You are hacking their website as we speak!" It's a fraternal order seeking to change the country's political landscape."

"No surprise there. You are just spouting out what is on the website—aimed at recruiting young white males that are frustrated with the way our government and society are being run."

"We just want things the way they used to be, but that's a different subject for another time. Other Brother is obviously what it appears to be; however, a secret society lies at the heart of it, operating behind the organization. My father is the founder of Other Brother and the leader of the cult, Other Brother's inner circle. They have created a plan to get the country 'back on track' and are implementing it right now...as we speak!"

"What you're telling me is that Other Brother is responsible for the surge in terrorist activity in this City and other major cities in the United States in the past few months?"

"Only the ones that fulfill 'The Agenda'."

"You realize we must verify all this with the FBI and Homeland Security."

"I hope you do. Then maybe you will..." Suddenly, a rumble was heard outside the interrogation room, and explosions and shouting were heard from beyond the door to the hallway. A few objects hit the ground and started releasing tear gas into the air. Dwight immediately got up from the table. "We've got to get you out of here."

"It's them...I told you it wouldn't take too long... They will level this whole place if they have to."

"Well then, we had better get a move on!" The hallway had zero visibility, and laser sites cut through the smoke. That way was not an option. An alarm started to sound, and the building was being evacuated. With all his strength, Dwight took one of the chairs and threw it through the one-way mirror. Sharon and Jerry Mack had left it empty. There were two doors to the room. One went into the hall that was now filled with tear gas that was seeping into the interrogation room and under the door of the observation room. The other doorway leads to the parking garage. Kyle went through the window first and stayed with Dwight. He felt his chances of staying alive were better with help. Dwight climbed through. They were going through the observation room door when they could hear glass shattering in the hallway and the interrogation room. They ran as fast as they could down a corridor. They hurried past several processing areas that were abandoned. The alarms were loud and clear. Fortunately, everyone was successfully evacuated from those office cubicles. Kyle and Dwight were not seen among the crowd spilling out of the precinct. They rushed into the parking garage in search of an exit. Dwight and Kyle had made it to the parking garage when several black, unmarked vehicles screeched to a halt right in front of the entrance, stopping the men in their tracks. Men in dark suits began to exit and crouch down behind the SUVs, positioning their weapons and zeroing in on anything that came their way. More were walking around, casing the perimeter, looking for the men. Just then, Dwight looked around and saw a navy crown Victoria with police plates pulled up just over a half-wall. Dwight told Kyle to leap.

Sharon sped off. Traffic was congested. She ignored all of the stop lights and crosswalks, praying that no one or anything would get in the way of their escaping the clutches of Other Brother. Where she was going, she didn't know. She was just trying to ditch the goons at full speed. Dwight and Kyle bounced around the back seat like children in the back of a 1970s station wagon with no seat belts. Sharon just kept driving —sharp turn after sharp turn. One dark SUV moved in behind them and began to pick up speed. Sharon's heart beat even faster as she tried to lose him. Another vehicle tried to cut them off, but she managed to use the oncoming traffic to get in their way. Finally, after about 25 minutes of non-stop fast and fancy stunt driving, they caught a glimpse of salvation. An on-ramp to the highway would be their way out, if they could break free of the chase. She heads toward the on-ramp, and the four

SUVs move into both lanes. The front two vehicles rolled down their windows, and one gunman was taking his position through the sunroof. The two on the sides of the Black Escalades in front started firing at them. The popping of the shots rang out, startling the other drivers. Trying to avoid the chase, the other drivers quickly exited the highway or swerved into traffic traveling the other way. The roar of the cars made people fearful. They didn't expect a gun battle as part of their daily commute to home or work.

Dwight stayed in the back seat with Kyle. Dwight still had his reservations about Kyle's trustworthiness. Kyle kept thinking that if Other Brother didn't kill him, this car chase might. Sharon hits a dip at an intersection, and a hubcap decides to detach from the car. The front of the car hits the pavement with a force that would have shattered the radiator of a normal car. But she kept on. They had to keep Kyle safe until they could find a safe place to get clarity. After several unsuccessful attempts to apprehend our unlikely trio of fugitives, the two front vehicles begin increasing their speeds to 70 miles per hour. A few more shots hit the quarter panel of their car and startled Sharon. She swerved into the fast lane and increased her speed to 75 miles per hour. Traffic held steady, keeping up with all of the vehicles in pursuit. Dwight, Sharon, and Kyle were in the lead car. The two vehicles in the back moved in closer, swerving to weave in and out, as if traffic were standing still.

The two gunmen were still taking shots at Dwight and Sharon, who were reaching speeds of 85 miles per hour and weaving in and out like they were riding in a Formula One race car. Then, the unthinkable happened. The highway began to turn south, and the gunman accidentally hit a different car going in the same direction as the chase. The driver was struck with a bullet and flew forward onto the steering wheel. The weight of his torso pulled the car to the left until it spun around and flipped twice in the air. It crashed down on top of several other cars going 65-70 miles per hour. Traffic came to a screeching halt and began to pile up on this particular stretch of highway. As the body count kept increasing. Sharon realized that if she didn't bring this chase to an end, the body count and the cost of the damage caused by this unrelenting pursuit would continue to rise. One by one, cars were piling up on the highway. Sharon began looking for a street sign that could enable them to get off the highway unseen by the assassins pursuing them. They were heading away from the city, into the lake country. Trees were becoming the predominant landscape now. Soon, they will be out of the metro area. Just as Sharon read a sign with an off-ramp, she thought of a plan to cause a distraction and exit the highway. Just at that moment, she could see the SUV pull up to her window, and inside was one of the gunmen pointing a 35 mm High Point at her face. She let out a totally unprofessional scream and slammed on the brakes. The car started "fishtailing" to a stop. Sharon made a quick steer to the left and quickly exited the highway at a speed of 86 m.p.h. The brakes were unresponsive, so Sharon had to improvise. She reached under the dashboard and pulled the emergency brake, which caused the car to slow much faster. The vehicle stopped right at the entrance of a used car dealership. They pulled in and waited. Then, all of a sudden, Sharon could see smoke rising from the car's sides. There was a burning smell. Dwight told everybody to get out and run towards the convenience store. All three poured out of the car and bolted for the Circle "K" Store Entrance. They were three paces from the automatic sliding glass doors when they could hear the EXPLOSION!! The sky started to rain shattered glass. The three of them turned around to look at the destruction that was happening behind them.

"They're gonna know we're here. We'd better keep moving," Dwight said as calmly as he could. His determination inspired the other two to move faster. Sure enough, the evil henchmen looked up in the sky and saw the pillar of smoke coming from the dealership, but Dwight, Sharon, and Kyle left the convenience store and headed for Kyle's father's cabin just 6 miles up the road. They commandeered a Trailblazer and made their getaway. They lost sight of the other vehicles and sighed that they had given them the slip. And with a normal speed, like the one posted on the sign at the side of the road, they just kept driving. They eased their way to a stop. Before them was a quaint little cabin made of logs and a forest green roof. It was very rustic-looking. It was obviously a hunting cabin.

"We will hold up here until we can figure this out."

"I feel like we won't have much time before those guys from Other Brother find us."

"One of us will be the lookout while the other talks to Kyle about his involvement and possible strategy to keep us alive."

"I'll take the first shift."

Kyle was in a large room with rustic furnishings, red plaid blankets, and thick wool curtains. Mounted on the cabin walls were prize bucks and large fish from all over the United States. There was a large fireplace in the middle of the far wall. Decorated with family photos and hunting trophies. Kyle was sitting in a large, dark plum-colored wing-back chair. He was staring at the empty fireplace. He had a neutral expression on his face and just stared. He was surely in shock from the car chase and the possibility of being killed. He thought about Casandra Davis and David lying in bed, soaked in their wounds. He thought about the lifeless body of his best friend and found that he would figure out how to bring his buddy justice. Dwight entered the room, gently crossed over to the other chair on Kyle's other side, and tried to mimic his expressionless face. There was a moment of silence as both men stared into the dark void, the empty fireplace before them. They took this time to "right themselves," pause, and go forward with the conversation about the case.

"Well, Kyle, now that we ditched the goons, why don't you tell me what you know about the death of Miss Casandra Davis and David Kinsingsworth?"

"Why don't you tell me what you know about Cassy...You think I don't know who you are, but I do. Cassy mentioned you several times during our conversation. You two had a "thing" years ago. I don't think she ever really got over you. Why do you think I surrendered to you? I knew you would have the empathy I needed to understand me...I mean to really understand what happened."

"I can't pretend I don't know what you are talking about, Kyle, but that was long ago. I have married a beautiful woman and have two lovely children."

"Okay, I get it. Listen to me when I tell you your breakup with Cassy drove her crazy!"

"Crazy how?"

"Only you can understand this because you have history with a woman like Cassy."

"Don't you mean Jimmy Rantor?" Sharon added as she entered the room. "The coast is clear as of right now. I'm Sorry. I couldn't help overhearing. "Dwight and Kyle looked up at Sharon when she entered the room, and silence fell over them. They felt, "This is a conversation we would rather keep private." Kyle looked at Dwight, not wishing to slight the female detective, Sharon. On the other hand, Kyle didn't want to be judged for what he was about to confess to Dwight. He knew that with Dwight's experience with trans females, he would listen to Kyle's statement with total impartiality. Kyle felt safe discussing his relationship with Casandra Davis in private.

Dwight understood that Kyle was a 6'2" tall college athlete. He had beautiful women vying for his attention all the time. He was blonde with "Boy-Next-Door" charm. His clear blue eyes attracted a wide variety of beautiful females, and his tastes were about as varied as the women who came onto him. In David Kinsingsworth's case, he discovered that his taste in sexual partners was not just limited to the female gender. David was the one who convinced Kyle to admit that he was bisexual. With his options laid out before him, the one that stole his heart was her. As he spoke of his attraction to Casandra's extraordinary nature and how her personality and demeanor seduced him into liking her, Dwight had flashbacks of his own experiences with her. Though Dwight decided to sit in silence, he could feel the words about her work magic into his heart. A familiar longing began to unlock and open up inside of him as it did in the beginning.

Dwight's flushed expression was the commonality Kyle needed to continue his statement with an unabashed, judgment-free language that only other men like Dwight could relate to and understand. Kyle talked about David with an affection in his voice that Dwight could identify with, although Dwight's tastes were definitely different than Kyle's. Dwight was only attracted to women. However, he did not expect a trans woman to turn his head. He had thoughts about trans women before, and he had to deal with these "night-time seductresses" in his dealings as a member of the police force. However, nothing could have prepared him for her. She was perfect, in form and function. She operated her feminine wiles with precision and grace. Every detail about her was executed with forethought and creativity. The residual sorrow made our detective confused, shaken up, and void when she left. She wasn't the only one damaged in the breakup. Dwight hasn't been the same since. Our detective could not "place the rock back the same way," forever altering the landscape of his "garden of life." Dwight denies it, but it changed him. Kyle knew it, and Sharon knew it. With a sadness in his heart, Dwight rose from his chair, stood at the fireplace with his back toward Kyle, and hung his head. Kyle knew the meaning of Dwight's moment of silence. Kyle hung his head too and contemplated the shared experience of grief. Dwight's grief stemmed from Cassy being murdered by Kyle. Kyle's grief is from a shared breakup with the very same person.

"It doesn't matter now. What matters is making sure that you face justice."

"You still think I killed her and David—my best friend."

"David was more than a friend, wasn't he?"

"When we first met, we were lovers for a time. That ended, but we remained best friends, especially after Cassy came into the picture. He started dating her first. They were hot for each other. I will admit I was jealous of them, or him-how much fun they had being together."

"Is that why you did it?"

"I AM TELLING YOU I DIDN'T DO IT!! That night, when I walked in on them, in bed together, they were already dead."

"Already dead? What do you mean?"

"Yes! I left in disgust. They had broken up! Cassy wanted David to marry her. David was just playing around. He never had plans on having anything permanent with her. At least that's what he said to me, but I LOVED HER! With everything I had. After Cassy and I broke up, I was devastated. I never wanted to see or date another person for the rest of my life. I didn't think I was going to be okay. David's mother noticed how depressed I was, so she gave me the number of her family therapist and suggested that I needed to talk to someone—process what I was feeling healthily. I thought she was full of shit, but I felt this bottomless feeling of loss growing inside me and I had to do something, so when Cassy and I broke up I was done."

"Wait...family therapist?"

"Yes."

"Did David go to this therapist also?"

"I imagine he did. It was good for him. He always seemed okay, no matter what was going on. Even sketchy situations never seemed to faze him. He always knew how to get out of them."

"You wouldn't happen to have the contact information on the family shrink, would you?" Kyle pulled out his phone and opened up his contact list.

"Yeah, here it is...Leslie Ross... Here is the number."

Dwight "old-school" pulled out a pen and small memo pad and wrote down the number of the Kinsingsworth family therapist. All of a sudden, Dwight heard something...faint in the distance. It was the rustling of leaves and the crunching of gravel. Someone in a vehicle was approaching and getting closer to the cabin. Sharon rushed into the room and told the two men that Other Brother had found them and they had better get out of the cabin. They escaped out the back door and ran into the woods to a small boat house. Sharon and Dwight exited first. Sharon turned around and noticed that Kyle didn't follow them. She turned to Dwight. "KYLE'S GETTING AWAY!!" In the distance, echoing through the trees, the detectives could hear Kyle's voice. Dwight could barely make out what he was saying. He kept repeating the two words over and over again until they couldn't be heard anymore. Dwight was out of breath. Sharon had slowed her pace to a brisk walk. She caught up to Dwight, and they stopped to catch their breath.

"Could you make out any of that?"

"It sounded like 'she's alive'. She's alive."

"I think he is talking about Cassy."

"When he was sighted, he was visiting someone at the hospital. Maybe this "sick friend" can answer some questions for us."

"If we can get to the nearest town and find transport back to the city, I will head down to the hospital and see who Kyle was visiting."

"It might be difficult, the nurse on duty said that he had brought in a 'Jane Doe' and was checking in on her when he was spotted by the staff at Mercy Hospital."

"Interesting, my gut tells me that it wasn't a Jane Doe."

"You think it's our missing Cassy Davis!"

"Just a hunch. Let's hurry and get back." They could hear Other Brother's henchmen getting close. The yelling at each other while triangulating their position told Dwight and Sharon that Other Brother had not yet gotten a visual on the two detectives, and they were not pursuing Kyle. Once again, Kyle had gotten away. Dwight and Sharon carefully made their way through the brush. They tried to stay quiet and out of sight. Sharon motioned to Dwight to look ahead at the hill they were approaching. At the bottom, there was a two-lane road. It was freshly paved, which meant it led back to the city. They might be able to find a way back to town and call for transport. Dwight started down the hill and headed to the road. Just then, a shot rang out and hit Sharon in the back of the arm. She went down with a thud. The sound and the rustle of leaves made Dwight turn around. He anxiously climbed back up the hill to where his partner lay in pain amid the leaves and various ground cover.

Dwight rushed to her aid. She was struck in the back of the arm and was bleeding heavily. Dwight had to get her to safety as soon as he could. He picked her up and slid down the hill to the road with her slung over his shoulder.

A navy pickup with Illinois plates was driving past them when he saw Dwight carrying Sharon on his shoulder and motioning for help. The driver pulled over and asked where they were headed. Dwight showed his badge and mentioned that his partner had been hit and needed immediate medical attention. The man was happy to volunteer to take them to Mercy Hospital. Dwight placed Sharon on his lap. She was unconscious. Her body was limp from blood loss. But her pulse said that she was fighting to stay alive. Dwight took a piece of cloth from the driver's glove box and tightly wrapped her arm. It seemed to temporarily stop the hemorrhaging. However, the light slap on her face and calling her name did nothing to revive her. His only hope was the heartbeat he felt pulsing under the tips of his two fingers. He closed his eyes. When he opened his eyes again, he noticed a little black box with a few dials and a bright red light. The digital readout on the front of it signaled to Dwight that it was a Citizens Band Radio.

"Is that a CB radio under your dash?"

"Yes...and it picks up police bands."

"May I use it to call ahead and let them know we're coming?"

"By all means, brother...here, I'll turn it to the police band, seein' that you got your hands full and all."

"Thank you, sir, I really appreciate the help."

"This is Detective Dwight Hussleman with Chicago PD! I am en route to Mercy Hospital with Officer Sharon Kastle. She is wounded. I repeat, officer down...en route to Mercy Hospital."

"This is the Chicago Sheriff's Department. We have received your distress call and have alerted Mercy Hospital of your arrival. Do you have an ETA?"

"We should be arriving in about 20 minutes, traffic permitting. I want to let you know my location, but I don't know what highway we are on."

"Sir... We are on State Highway 65 going towards Chicago. Mile marker 246."

"Thank you! We are on State Highway 65 going towards Chicago. Mile marker 246!" Dwight repeated.

"Roger that! We are sending a police escort now."

"We are in a navy-blue pickup truck with Illinois plates 346-RTO."

"Copy That! Stay on course, we are almost to you!"

"Hussleman out..." With a four-car police escort, it wasn't long before the two detectives and their driver pulled up to the hospital entrance. The rush toward the vehicle drew a lot of onlookers as they lifted Sharon out of Dwight's arms onto the gurney, where they wheeled her into emergency surgery. Dwight felt confident in their speed and efficiency. Somehow, he knew that they weren't gonna let her die.

He took the elevator to the front desk and approached the nurse on duty. She was very young, in her mid-twenties, and just out of med school. She wore colorful printed scrubs with white shoes and a name tag that read, "Hello, I am Nurse Sarah." Dwight approached her and immediately flashed his winning smile, along with his badge. She was naturally intimidated by Dwight's confidence as he asked his personal questions about the patients there. These were questions that she wasn't at liberty to answer. Just then, another older nurse, just as confident as our detective, recognized Dwight from the chase in the emergency room.

"Well, look who it is...You're famous around here. How can I help you? I have some nice patients you can leap over and some gurneys you can ride up and down the hallway! We cleared it just for you! How can I help you today?"

# Chapter Ten-Call me Miss Ross

Still in shock that his smiling, young, college-age nurse was replaced by a 'Helga-style' nurse ratchet—with no professional manner and no regard for the male species. Nevertheless, Dwight remained professional. Undaunted, Dwight had an agenda and understood that he had little time to find her. He was eager to prove whether or not his hunch was true —that Casandra was somewhere in the hospital being treated for her wounds. Dwight had no idea that his intuition was correct. Not only that, but Dwight would discover more clues related to the case. Clues that will, finally, clear up some things about the murder, the assassination, and Other Brother.

"Yes, I wanted to come by and apologize for all of the mayhem I may have caused, and I hope I didn't get anyone hurt in the process. I was only doing my duty. Thank you for the tip. It proved to be very helpful. I was attempting to apprehend the suspect and bring him in for questioning." Dwight hoped that if he used his charm and engaged the nurse directly, she might allow him to proceed with his search for Miss Davis.

"If I remember it correctly, looks like the perp is the one that got the upper hand," She mused.

"It did appear that he had me pinned."

"And in a choke hold,"

"...um. Look, I have very little time. The gentleman who had me pinned, after chasing him through your waiting area, said that he brought in a Jane Doe. She would have been of Polynesian descent. She is about 5'6". She would have been treated for excessive bleeding of the neck and maybe some minor flesh wounds on her torso. You wouldn't happen to know anything about that, would you?"

"The only patient that was brought in for those kinds of injuries was a male. Goes by the first name Jimmy. He was a local performer here in the Chicago area. At least that's what he has been telling the night staff."

"Is he still here? Can you tell me his room number?"

"Now, Hold on, Cowboy! We don't just hand out patient information willy-nilly. We need a search warrant or some sort of official decree to even get near our psych patients."

"Psych... patient?"

"Yes, and that's all I can tell you without a summons or a warrant issued by the court."

"Thank you. I will have that for you shortly."

"You do that, Stud." Nurse Athena Brotherton gave Dwight a flirtatious glance. She turned to the right and lowered her head with five rapid blinks. Then, a pause. Then, she looks up at the handsome investigator and blinks two more times, slowly. This display was aimed at enticing our detective. However, he felt his shoulders tighten and his heart beating inside his chest. He decided to exit the front desk area before he completed the gag reflex. She didn't care. She decided it was his loss and returned to filing patient records. Dwight could have easily stood his ground and demanded that she release the information. But since he already had access to the hospital, he thought he could wander around and look for someone more 'helpful' to point him toward the missing queen. He started with the hospital directory sign. The Psychiatric Ward was listed on the sign alongside all of the other departments on the third floor. So, Dwight nervously hopped on the elevator.

Throughout the elevator ride, Dwight anticipated seeing the lost love of his life. What would she look like? Would she greet him with a smile and a quip? Or would she meet his gaze with disdain and regret? All the questions would be answered in what seemed to be an eternity—floor two. Dwight recalled when they went to an ice cream stand in one of Chicago's beautiful neighborhoods. Cassy wanted to discuss the possibility of living there with the man of her dreams. Dwight laughed at the thought of them moving in together, at how preposterous it was for him to consider such an arrangement. It was his mistake. He realizes that now. The laugh broke her heart, not what he expected. It was a different time then. He has regretted it ever since. Today's world is more open and progressive, but feelings remain as intense as ever. Her life would have been safer, and his life would have been more enriched. Together, they would have conquered the world. The issue of children did cross his mind. Misty later fulfilled that item on his bucket list. It's a second chance, but it's now exponentially complicated with a wife and kids who didn't exist before Dwight and Cassy met.

When the third-floor doors opened, he noticed a difference in temperature and mood. The atmosphere on the third floor is a balmy 70 degrees. What is more alarming is the change in mood. When Dwight stepped off the elevator, he sensed a presence behaving like a disturbed hostess, welcoming the detective with open arms and a smile as if to say: "Welcome to the third floor—the Psych Ward. "He walks down a long hallway to a corridor enclosed by double doors and a small sign: "300-313." An arrow pointed to those rooms. The thought of peeking into 13 doorways and explaining himself 13 times did not appeal to him. He waited for a few minutes. Two men came into the hallway. He immediately drew their attention. They moved towards him. Dwight ducked into a closet and found an old lab coat. He put it on and stepped out into the hall. The two men dressed in all-white polyester two-piece outfits with short sleeves and long pants approached. Dwight caught their eyes once more, and they asked him if they could assist him. Dwight claimed to have a patient on this floor and needed to consult with them. They showed him to Cassy's room. The light was dim as if to indicate that she was sleeping. He asked if she was awake. They didn't know. He dismissed them and turned towards the door.

The walls had a calming effect. The room had blue-grey painted walls. The bed was against the wall, and Dwight could hear a soft voice speaking to the air. It was a prayer. She was asking for guidance and forgiveness. Dwight recalled that when they were together, she would pray for a blessing to be bestowed upon them both for a long and healthy relationship. Maybe the answer was, "No, for one of you is not ready for this life with the other." Still playing the odds, she persevered, hoping for the day when he would change his mind. Much like she was doing now. Dwight lightly steps into the room. Too late now. Silent and still, he doesn't say a word. He tries not to breathe. She ends the prayer abruptly and listens to the silence of the room. An eternity goes by. Dwight and Casandra are still paralyzed; seconds turn into eons. Out of respect for all that Casandra had been through. As fate would have it, a nurse with a tray of little cups walked by where Dwight was standing. Each cup contained colorful little pills. She was making her rounds.

"Sir...Sir! Visiting hours ended at 8 pm." Dwight didn't move. "Sir! Did you not hear me? Besides, to see a patient on this floor, you must fill out an appointment request and specify the date and time you would like to see them." Dwight nodded in compliance and began to exit the room.

"Let him stay, Debbie," Came a soft and sad voice from beyond the curtain, "He's Leslie's assistant. He's just checking on me." Cassy started to cough. Then she began to move around on the hospital bed, and the jostling stirred up concern with the nurse. She set her tray down, walked over to the drawn curtain, and stepped through. She disappears for a few minutes to ensure Miss Davis is comfortable. She asked if Cassy wanted Dwight to be in her room. Cassy nodded. The nurse didn't say a word. She picked up her tray and resumed making her rounds. Once again, the silence flooded the room. Dwight walked up to the curtain and stood with his two hands on the opening. He lowered his head. There was nothing he could do but take a deep breath and... walk through.

"You must know that I am not your therapist's assistant," he uttered through the closed curtain. "I know," she returned. There was a soft light next to the bed. Dwight stood tall and strong like a statue. Cassy was gobsmacked at the sight standing before her. Dwight was at a loss for words. All of their memories rushed to greet him. He could not process them all at once. He just smiled with a glossy-eyed expression. There was so much to say and no time. She pulled herself back. Her memories came rushing back to her. How can you be angry at someone whom you love? No matter how much they hurt you? Cassy was strong and independent, but it was Dwight. The love of her life was standing in front of her. The goal, after all, is to find out the truth about what happened to her and who is involved. She blinked twice. A signal for Dwight to "break the ice."

"Why did you come?"

"You have been through a traumatic experience. I came to get your statement."

"Did you go to the morgue first? Then the Psych ward? Or, did you flip a coin?" There was no change in the pitch or pace of her voice. Yet, the whole meaning of the statement was felt. It was a dig at the time that had elapsed since they last saw each other. Dwight approached the bed and touched her hand. He could feel the trembling. The fear had gripped her in so many different ways that she was surprised by the involuntary shaking of her hands. The wee hours of the morning were rapidly approaching, and he could feel her getting tired. He decided to let her sleep. His questioning could wait a few more hours.

He went back to the desk. There was a shift change happening among the nurses. He noticed an older woman approaching him. She had a name tag that said 'Dr. L. Ross, Psychologist.' She held some files in one hand and a cup of coffee in the other. At first, she went to the desk and didn't see Dwight standing there, still wearing the lab coat. He just kept looking at her, trying to make eye contact. She was busy updating the staff on the day's agenda. His patience, however, was paying off. She looks at Dwight and asks him if he needs assistance. After removing the lab coat and pulling out his badge, He asked if they could speak privately. Dr. Ross immediately became concerned, yet his request did not alarm her. She asked him about his business with her, and he explained his situation. He told her that the reason they hadn't met sooner was that they had just realized that Miss Davis was not a "Jane Doe" but one of the victims in a murder case involving the Mayor's son. It took some to convince her, but Dr. Leslie Ross agreed to let Dwight conduct his investigation. As long as it doesn't interfere with Cassy's treatment under the guidance of Miss Ross, Dwight is welcome to come back in the evening after Miss Davis awakens.

"Dr. Ross, with all due respect, we are quickly running out of time. I must ask Jimmy some questions about the investigation."

"Visiting hours are from 8 am to 8 pm. I can make an exception in this case."

"Thank you, I appreciate your cooperation." Dwight turned around and walked back to Jimmy's/ Casandra's room. He was rudely interrupted by an alarm in the hallway and staffers scrambling in and out of Jimmy's room. Dwight started running towards the room. It was Casandra they were wheeling out. He watched in disbelief as they quickly moved the gurney past him. Down the hall, past the front desk, and disappearing through the double doors. He walked into the room to see for himself. The bed was in disarray, and there was blood on the rails and the sheets. His heart figuratively stopped beating and sank deeper into his chest. His eyes started to turn red, and his face? Flushed with anguish. A nurse walked by. Dwight stopped her and asked about the cardiac arrest alarm. Out of breath and hurried, she explained that the alarm was for the patient. They suffered a cardiac arrest, and they are moving them to the ICU. "Since the first day they were admitted as a 'Jane Doe,' they have been on a roller coaster ride of flat-lining and then leveling out at sundown."

"That's why I told you that you won't be able to see Jimmy until sundown. I wasn't trying to be mean. That's when he transitions into Casandra." She nodded at Debbie, the nurse. Debbie immediately started running after Jimmy's gurney.

"You see, Jimmy Rantor suffers from a condition called Cognitive Dissociative Disorder. He has more than one person living inside him."

"We need to talk. I need to understand what I am dealing with before continuing the investigation. How about a cup of coffee?"

"My Mother always taught me: 'If a handsome man offers to buy you coffee, you say yes!'" They made their way across the street to the small coffee shop on the corner and found a quiet couch in the back so they could talk freely about Jimmy's condition. Dwight paid for the coffee and carried it to a cozy little spot for Miss Ross. She was very demure in Dwight's presence. She turned on a small lamp on a table next to a tan leather couch. The softly lit space lent itself well to talking frankly about sensitive subject matter, like CDD and how it relates to murder. "You know, even after all of my years on the force, I still feel awkward about talking about things such as death, in general, and specifically, murder."

"I know what you mean. Some things shouldn't be commonplace for a therapist to hear, but to this day, I have difficulty discussing them with patients. Don't worry. The minute it stops affecting us is the minute we should be worried. Very worried," Leslie added, "Jimmy's case is unusual and unique in all of its complexities. Normally, in cases like this, we would try to integrate all personalities and create the whole person. In Jimmy's case, I am unsure if that would be a good idea. If we try to integrate Casandra and Jimmy's separate personas, it could kill one or both of them. The implications of one surviving and the other not surviving could devastate Jimmy."

"In what way?"

"Well, for example, there is 'survivor's guilt.' Quite common in veterans who survive a war. However, their comrades were not as fortunate. Leslie takes a sip of coffee, "They have such guilt and remorse that it can manifest in tragic ways. When the guilt wins, it can result in self-inflicted mutilation, bottomless depression, and some victims even unalive themselves. What I'm saying is, if we can even(successfully) integrate Casandra into Jimmy, Jimmy's injuries could be too irreparable for him to survive—killing them both. By the same token, if we integrate Jimmy into Casandra, Casandra may have unresolved grief over the loss of Jimmy."

"It could also mean a gender reassignment, which could have societal and social ramifications, which could lead to more trauma."

"Exactly, so, for the moment, we are taking a step back and only going to observe his reaction to the treatments. We can also treat the immediate residual trauma," Leslie changes the subject.

"Dwight, I agreed to help you get the answers you need to move forward in your investigation. I was wondering if we could participate in an exchange of information about Jimmy and this case. It might help us help him. Everyone wins."

"Okay, shoot."

"Well, what can you tell me about where he came from? Where does he perform? His daily routine? Things like that." Dwight opened up and told Dr. Ross everything he could without revealing details about the actual murder or his actual involvement with the subject. He didn't mention anything about Kyle and the Other Brother Organization. During the conversation, Dwight had to use the bathroom. He went to the urinal, and a poster advertising the Lido was on the wall. Underneath the announcement was an array of snapshots of the nightclub's entertainers. Right in the middle was a picture of Casandra Davis. He made sure no one was looking, and without wasting any time, he ripped it off the wall, folded it up, and stuffed it inside his jacket. He walked back to the area where Leslie was sitting.

"So, how exactly were you able to find out that our Jane Doe was actually Jimmy Rantor—Jimmy Raymond Rantor," Dwight said, opening up a new subject to wrap their minds around.

"Don't you mean Jimmy Anton Rantor? That's the name that he gave the records office."

"That may be. However, DNA testing revealed that his name, given to him at birth, is indeed Jimmy Raymond Rantor."

"Interesting. I wonder why Jimmy wouldn't want to give his real name to the records office."

"To avoid paying the bill?"

"Probably, in some cases, to a CDD patient, a middle name can be an 'Easter egg', a clue to something hidden in the game, the movie, or (in this case) the mind of the patient. It is possible that inside Jimmy, there could be more entities than just the ones he is allowing us to interact with."

"If so, I might be able to talk to Jimmy's other entities that may have witnessed the murder and provide answers as to who did it and why!"

"Hold on, Dwight. You need to be extremely careful. If you are doing that, you should have his therapist present."

"Okay then. I am meeting you tonight! We'll do it together." Dwight had to leave and check on Sharon to see how her recovery was going. "I have to go. See you in Jimmy's room at 7:30 pm sharp."

"Thanks for the coffee!" Dwight's only response was a quick left arm raised in the air, with a hand stretched up to the sky, as a farewell gesture. He navigated traffic to get across the street, back to the hospital, and Sharon's room. She was watching TV. She was brandishing a freshly dressed bandage on her arm and a lavender hospital gown. She was sitting up and bored. She immediately cheered up at the sight of her partner entering the room. "Well, I am not really watching anything in particular." She's wildly pointing a black handheld object into the air and waving it around as if it were going to bring something enriching to her life while she remained bedridden. "How's our Jane Doe doing?"

"Turns out she is suffering from post-traumatic stress disorder..."

"Not surprising..."

"Well, this might surprise you. As a result of a lifetime of cruelty and abuse—both physical, mental, and emotional—Casandra/ Jimmy has developed Cognitive Dissociative Disorder."

"You mean multiple personalities?"

"Yes, and their given name is Jimmy Rantor—our missing Casandra Davis!"

"YES!" Sharon exclaimed, elated that they finally got a break and could start getting answers. She wonders if Jimmy/Casandra knows the whereabouts of this elusive, nefarious Antonio. After their encounter with Kyle, Sharon just couldn't believe that Kyle could want Casandra dead, especially after the way that she heard him talk about her. "Their therapist, Leslie Ross, explained it to me. I am supposed to meet her at 7:30 pm to question Jimmy/Casandra about the murder of David Kinsingsworth."

"Why so late?"

"Apparently, their condition is so severe that it affects their physiology as well, and the only time that I will be able to see her is when the sun goes down, which will be around 7:30 pm tonight!"

"Interesting. Do you think that Miss Davis will be able to offer any insight into David's murder or Other Brother?" Then, as Sharon Kastle flipped to a local news channel, the face of former Mayor Kinsingsworth's widow was on the screen, speaking to a crowd of reporters. She was tearful and graceful. Sharon and Dwight could not believe what was happening. "Turn up the volume," Dwight said. The crowd was there to hear Mrs. Kinsingsworth speak about her son's and husband's deaths. She politely and carefully answered the reporter's questions. She thanked the Chicago police force for their diligent efforts. She announced a one-hundred-thousand-dollar reward for any information leading to the apprehension of the person or group responsible for her son's death. Shocking news came in the form of the finale of her speech. Candace Kinsingsworth announced that once this investigation is over and her son's killer has been brought to justice, she is making plans to run for office and carry on the work of her husband in honor of his memory and the Kinsingsworth family legacy. Her grief and determination were a potent mix, and the crowd was electrified by her sentiment. She would make a formidable politician. Just then, a knock came at Sharon's room door. The door was open, so the person knocking was just being polite. Sharon's attending physician, Dr. Grant, brought her release papers. She was free to go. She got her things and met Dwight in the lobby of the main hospital. The wound was still fresh, so Dwight assigned her a light-duty task that she could manage. He wrote out a laundry list of supplies that Dwight would need. He hands her a piece of paper and gives her strict instructions on what to buy."I need them for my interview with Miss Davis tonight. Can you get these things for me?"

"No problem. I will go to the corner store, buy the things, and drop them off at the hospital by 7:30 pm."

"Perfect. Thank you. See you soon!" Sharon knew what Dwight was up to. While not holding PhDs in psychology, detectives must study introductory psychology as it pertains to their role as investigators. Sharon understood that Dwight's subject must be as comfortable as possible if the interview process was to be successful. This strategy was designed to encourage the suspect or victim to open up and readily provide the necessary answers. Yes, he sent Sharon to pick up some essentials for Miss Davis. Cassy could wear makeup, put on a dress, and feel more like herself. In the process, Miss Davis will be more willing to cooperate with detectives. Perhaps she knows who Antonio is, his involvement in the case, and his affiliation with Other Brother. Like the Trevor Whitney case, Cassy will be the key that blows the case wide open.

Dwight knew it, and he was sure that if Casandra stayed in the hospital for very long, the Others would know it too and want to eliminate the Polynesian princess before she could expose who they were to the world. Dwight had to have a plan.

In the meantime, Miss Davis was making plans of her own... Dwight was drinking a cup of coffee in the cafe across the street when he noticed that the sun pounding the pavement was beginning to fade. He had better make his way back to the hospital. He gently pushed in his chair and wiped the tabletop with his coffee napkin. He paused to look at the napkin, and the motion of wiping the table made his mind flash back to his wife. Misty wiped the countertops at home just the same. Dwight thought about Misty's sacrifices over the years—being the wife of a detective couldn't have been easy. She practically raised their two children all by herself. He started to choke up. His heart was hurting for her and the kids. "I'm going to miss you, Sweetheart," He whispered to the empty room.

# Chapter Eleven-Layers of Layers

Sharon shows up at the hospital carrying a tote with the requested items for Dwight, but she is not alone. Jerry Mack was walking beside her with more information. They both approached Dwight, bearing items of a completely different nature. While Sharon donned a bag of ladies' cosmetics, Jerry Mack had a file containing the toxicology report on the man who shot the Mayor and then ate the evidence. The SIM card from his phone had vital information on the origin of the hit. Dwight already had a hunch that Other Brother ordered it. He just needed proof. Jerry Mack didn't know exactly the details of where Dwight was headed in the investigation, but Jerry wasn't more than two steps away at any given moment.

"The Report found traces of a drug in his system," Dwight read out loud to everyone in the waiting area of the Psych Ward on the third floor, "Zoro Tropo Entropine."

"It was a party drug. It was first discovered in 2012 when ravers in New England were overdosing on it and winding up in the hospital by the hundreds," Leslie chimed in. She was pushing the gurney with Casandra on it. Cassy was leveling out and coming out of the induced coma. They were guiding her back to her room and hooking up the machines. Leslie then went to the nurses' station, where she was greeted by Nurse Debbie."I appreciate all this attention, really, but it isn't necessary. I feel fine." Casandra was as tough as she was beautiful. Dwight commandeered the bag from his partner and approached the Diva—bag in hand.

"I come bearing gifts," Dwight says, handing Cassy the bag, and she starts looking through it.

"Oh My Gosh! Thank you for this," she continued, looking at all the items in the bag. "I thought you might feel a little better if you could feel and look more like yourself."

"Dwight, that is so sweet of you to do that. You don't know how difficult it is to smuggle a good pair of slippers here, let alone the full 'LEFT CHEEK' cosmetic collection."

"I hope I did a good job picking out the shades."

"I'll make it work. Thanks again, Dwight."

"You're welcome; if it's okay with you, after you finish your beautification ritual, I would like to ask you some questions about the investigation."

"Sure. I'll be out in 'two shakes.'" Cassy bolted to the bathroom and closed the door. Dwight walked over to Sharon and Jerry. After talking with them, citing "too many cooks spoil the pot," he was able to convince Jerry and Sharon to go back to headquarters to research this psychotropic drug—Zoro Tropo Entropine. Sharon and Jerry left as Leslie entered the room. "Before I go, I wanted to let you know that there was a website on the SIM card. Its IP address was encrypted. It is the official website of Other Brother. You should check it out. There was also a list of instructions for the hit man assigned to take out the Mayor and his son. It was strangely specific, and our gunman carried out the instructions to a tee!"

"Great job, Jerry. I will get right on it. Right now, I need to take Miss Davis' statement."

"The common name is ZTE—also the acronym," Leslie began, "On the street, it is commonly referred to as ZETA. If you ask for ZETA, you pay 35 dollars, and you will get one little green pill. It is so small that you can hide it in the eraser of a pencil. It is ineffective when taken after ingesting any type of soda. It is highly addictive after the third dose. Two doses taken together can give the victim brain damage. Three doses taken at the same time can be fatal. You usually buy five at a time. In today's market, ZETA costs $100 for five doses. I've treated several ZETA addicts over the years. I've pioneered a state-of-the-art addiction treatment that takes four years to gain full recovery. The CDC did not see a happy ending, but we were making progress. All of a sudden, it disappeared off the face of the planet. No one was making it. Rumors flew about where it went. However, nobody could find it anywhere."

"Interesting." Although he was happy to hear this new information offered freely by a well-known psychologist, Leslie Ross, Dwight was focused on his interview with Casandra Davis and anxious to listen to what light she could shed on the case. Dwight noticed the door opening and the light turning off. Cassy had emerged from the bathroom like a butterfly from a cocoon. She was painted and picture-perfect. She paused while entering the room to see how the dress fit her curves. It was a perfect fit. Her expression changed from fear to confidence, just as Dwight had hoped. She looked up at the room. Dr. Leslie, Nurse Debbie, and Dwight were transfixed on the Diva as she glided to the recliner in the corner, gently floated down onto the seat, and crossed her legs at the ankles. "I'm ready if you are," Her eyes darted around the room. Dwight knew that she was already making plans and that his time was limited. She will lose faith in the process, or the sun will break over the horizon, and Dwight will have to wait until the following sundown.

"Okay, let's begin, "Dwight pulled an "old-school" tape recorder from his pocket and set it on the table next to Miss Davis. He glanced at Nurse Debbie and Dr. Leslie, politely asking them to leave the room so that he could make his inquiries without any distractions. Nurse Debbie complied by explaining that she had patients to visit and medications to administer. Leslie was a little more apprehensive—understandable, but unnecessary. She finally left, but Dr. Ross told Dwight that she wanted to listen to the tapes before Cassy's deposition goes in his report. Dwight said he would. With everyone out of the room except the two former lovers, Dwight suddenly forgot the first question he wanted to ask. There was an awkward pause, and Cassy finally looked him in the eye and made an observation that Dwight was not prepared to address.

"You seem different somehow. Married life must be agreeing with you."

"Cassy, with all you have been through, I shouldn't have abandoned you the way I did. I was stupid."

"That's a hell of an apology."

"We live in a different time now. Society and people in general are more accepting of alternatives to straight and gay relationships. I feel like some of the pressure to conform has been lifted. Pandora's Box has been opened, and there is no going back."

"Dwight, what are you talking about? Society is trying to 'put the lid back on Pandora's Box as we speak. It's just as bad as it ever was!"

"I'm saying you and I have been given a second chance to be together. REALLY together."

"With all that I have been through in my life, all the money and time I have spent trying to get men like you to respect me for who I am. I mean, I tried everything. I tried being a good girl. I tried being a slut. I tried being a man. I couldn't escape the fact that inside, I was female. Now that you have grown this new life—without me, I might add, I am supposed to thank the gods that you have finally come around? I don't know Dwight. It's a lot to process. You make it hard for me to be ladylike when I am angered and frustrated by society's treatment of us."

"You are a lady...don't make it hard for me to be a man right now," Dwight said, taking Cassy's hand into his. "We can figure this out together. I am here. Fate has brought us together again. It's time to be who we are and not worry about anything...but us."

With that, Dwight escorted Cassy to the darker side of the hospital room. The part that was not illuminated by the fluorescent light above the bed. His large fingers caressed hers, and he wrapped his hand around her hand and gently placed it on his chest. He was close enough to hear her exhale at the touch of his warmth. She noticed that underneath the exterior of this tough, hard-hitting detective was the excited heartbeat of a starry-eyed teenage boy. She smiles and lets her guard down. "Game on." Dwight thought to himself. When he turns on the charm, there isn't a woman within 500 feet of him that can resist it, and he is laying it on thick.

Dwight moved in close. The world did not exist. The fact that he could be "dancing with the Devil himself—wrapped up in a beautiful nightmare, didn't matter. He looked into Cassy's eyes. He searched for a clue that might lead to his next move.

"Are we dancing right now?"

"Yes, Cassy. We are."

"I don't understand really why I am even here. In this place. How did I get here?"

"Shh...It's okay. Did Dr. Ross not give you any details about your situation?"

"I only know what she is willing to tell me. I certainly didn't think we would see each other again. Not like this—not after so long."

"Cassy. I need you to open up to me. Can you do that?"

"First, tell me why I am here, cooped up in a Hospital and dancing with a homicide detective? I mean, the last thing I can remember was... David and I were..." She finished her sentence with a gasp. It was too late to stop it. Surprised and looking at Dwight, she became tense. However, she may be relaxed enough to be honest with Dwight. With the prospect of rekindling a feeling that has been dormant inside her for so long, she refrained from finishing her sentence for fear that it would kick Dwight out of romantics and into forensics. At a loss for words, she looks at Dwight for a clue as to what he knows about what happened that night. Both of them are remarkably intuitive, which makes games of "Cat and Mouse" impossible to win.

"Well, Dr. Ross asked me not to discuss why you are on the third floor. She fears that it will trigger a trauma response that could influence your current mental state," Dwight whispered delicately, face to face to Casandra, illuminated by the lone fluorescent light on the other side of the room.

"Great. Did Leslie mention when I might be released?"

"Shh...I need you to focus on me while I ask the questions. We have very little time before I have to go. Don't worry; I will return with more questions for you and answer all of your questions as well. Alright?"

"Fine."

They both continue swaying in the corner. Dwight is anticipating that he might have to inform her that David is dead. He moves in closer. He looks up at the ceiling. Then, he looks at her. She stares back at him. Her eyes tear up at the thought of what she is about to ask Dwight and the answer that he will have to give her. Waves of memories of that fateful night at Casandra's apartment start to rise. Tears start to flow. "I know that you and David shared a fondness for each other, and you were together the night that David was murdered."

"Then, you know more about the night I was brought here than I do."

"I can't give you any details while the investigation is going on, but I can tell you that we will catch whoever did this to you, Cassy, I promise."

"Oh, I don't doubt you. The Mayor has his top investigators competing for clues to solve that landmark case. Was Trevor Whitney not enough for you?" Her cynicism was palpable.

"You know, if it wasn't for THAT case, we wouldn't have met," He bumps her nose with his.

"Yeah. I was pretty beaten up that time."

"You healed nicely..."

"Not totally..." Cassy sobbed for a while in Dwight's arms. He strokes her hair to comfort her. For a brief moment, she was back at the Lido. Sitting on Dwight's lap, they laugh at the performers competing for the title 'Miss Amateur Queen.'

"I want to take you back to your apartment the night that David was killed."(record scratch) "Well, I don't remember much about that night. It was raining. David, 'out of the blue,' wanted to talk to me. He bribed the security guard and came to my dressing room."

"What happened next?"

"One thing led to another, and we wound up at my place, in bed, and having sex."

"David was about to, you know. I looked up at the doorway, and Kyle was standing at the end of the bed in the strobe of the storm. Kyle was heartbroken and holding a bouquet of pink roses and a ring. It was the biggest Diamond I had ever seen. Another flash, and he disappeared.

That flash knocked out the power, and I couldn't see where he went. I thought I had too much to drink, and I was hallucinating."

"Then he came back, didn't he?"

"How do you know that?"

"I am a detective...erp!" She laughed. Casandra was enjoying her time with him.

"Did Kyle return?"

"Kyle left in anger and disappointment. With all of the commotion from the storm, I didn't even hear him pounding on the door; even so, I wasn't about to ruin my moment with David to open the door for anybody. Then, out of nowhere, a knife plunges into David's back and throat."

"Did you see who it was that plunged the knife into David?"

"I closed my eyes to fake being dead. It worked. They left. I passed out and woke up in the hospital. So, I guess the answer is no—I didn't see them."

"You said they. You don't think it was Kyle?"

"I assumed it was, at first. I don't know for sure. I CAN'T be sure. I was hoping David would make it, but there was blood...mine...his...everywhere! I was so weak from the blood loss, I passed out."

"Why did you assume it was Kyle? What changed your mind?"

"I broke his heart. I thought he wanted revenge. He loved me and was willing to stake his own life for mine. I betrayed him." Cassy's emotions were taking over. Dwight's window was about to close. "I am not here to judge. I, too, have made bad decisions. Especially about me and you."

"I don't think Kyle did it. he is a Harvard wrestler. That knife should have pierced both of us. It was long enough. The person holding the knife was not strong enough to force it completely through. I'm no expert, but my instincts are spot on."

"What do you think of when I say the name Antonio?"

"The Janitor of the Lido? Antonio? Do you think he had something to do with David's murder?"

"I can't tell you that. Remember? At this point, anyone could be a suspect."

"Even me?"

"Anyone..." Dwight and Casandra stayed up all night talking. She told him she hadn't known Leslie very long, yet their interactions indicate that Dr. Ross may have known Cassy her whole life. They tried to go over details about her life, but after the Trevor Whitney attack, she basically has lost all memory of her past. She can't remember any names or significant events in her life. She can't remember dates—like her Birthday, the day she moved to Chicago, or even how she ended up in the Windy City. She remembers the Lido, Vidal Sassman, and the girls. Anything before that is blank to the point that she becomes ill when she tries to recall memories of her past. Dwight thought about the comment on Leslie Ross. Maybe it was time for another coffee session with the good Doctor. So, Dwight arranged for Doctor Ross to meet him for coffee and discuss Casandra's condition more deeply.

"It's true. Cassy has no recollection of anything, anyone, or anytime that happened before the attack by the rapist-Trevor Whitney." Leslie takes a sip of coffee—Colombian ground. And continued, "She moved to Chicago to escape the abuse of the man that his mother married after her father left.

His name was Marvin. She told me during a hypnosis session about an instance where the stepfather forced 13-year-old Jimmy Rantor to put his new bed together on his own. Well, Jimmy had never even touched a power tool. Judging from old photos of Jimmy, he couldn't have lifted the Hammer or the Drill to put the bed together properly anyway—the stepfather was setting him up for failure. He was beaten so severely that his jaw was dislocated, both eyes were swollen shut, and he was tied to a tree and left for dead for the next 24 to 48 hours. His next-door neighbor, Antonio, saw him there and cut him down. He nursed Jimmy's swollen eyes and took him to his house to seek refuge. They became best friends from then on."

"How close were they?"

"Antonio and Jimmy were inseparable. Jimmy often switched names with Antonio, and Antonio became Jimmy. They would mimic each other to a tee, like a game of tag. Jimmy loved him. He took Jimmy's virginity before he left."

"Antonio left? Where is he now?"

"Not sure. Rumor is that Antonio joined the military to keep from having to go to prison for petty crimes he committed around their hometown of Somerset, Missouri. He was strong in both mind and body. Jimmy says that he joined a Special Forces Unit in the Marines. He was an expert marksman."

"I would like to find this Antonio person and ask him some questions regarding Casandra Davis."

"Just be careful what you say to Cassy. Remembering makes her violently ill."

"Got it. What if Cassy reveals something about one of the personalities?"

"It's okay to address them as if they are real. To Casandra, they are real. Do not under any circumstances, ask any of her personalities about David or anyone related to the investigation, and her night at the apartment—in case she is still in shock or grief. What's remarkable is that you are the only person she hasn't blocked out from her past. She still remembers you and every detail of your time together."

"Cassy," Dwight called out to the dark room. Cassy had wandered to the window; she looked so beautiful in the moonlight. "Sky is getting dark...gonna storm."

"Where is Jimmy right now?"

"He is dying."

"Why is Jimmy dying?" Dwight knew full well that these were questions that he was forbidden to ask. "He wasn't hurt the night that David was murdered. Your wounds were superficial. So, what is the matter with Jimmy? Why is he dying?"

"Jimmy is trying to kill me, but I am stronger and tougher than he is." Her expression went blank. Her facial shape changed. No, she changed, like a shape-shifter in a science fiction novel. Then, like the turn of a page, she returned. Again, she stood before Dwight as if nothing had happened, "I don't feel well."

A crack of thunder boomed through the sky. A storm had begun to form. Dwight runs over to her and wraps her up in his arms. She is shaking. He looks at her, and she stares up at him. She is pleading for him to release her from this nightmare. He stays until the storm passes.

"It's just rain...not one flash of lightning. See?"

"Thank you for staying with me."

"Hey, are you hungry? There is a coffee shop across the street. I can at least score us some "JOE?"

"What d' ya say?" Cassy's only response was to grab Dwight's manly face and gently kiss him. It was a lovers' kiss. A kiss that sent shivers down his spine, "I would love some coffee," she said. Dwight takes a moment to process the kiss. He pauses. All the while, his eyes never leave hers, "Hang tight. I'll be right back." He flashes her his handsome smile and throws on his coat.

On his way to the coffee shop, he looks at his phone. It had been silent during Miss Davis' questioning. Sharon had called him several times and left several voicemails: "Dwight, this is Sharon. We need to talk. I have some information about the case that I can't share with you over the phone. If you receive this message, I need you to meet me somewhere so I can show you what I've found. Believe me, you'll want to hear this."

"Sharon, It's Dwight. What have you got?"

"Research on everyone associated with the case. I've conducted background checks, reviewed FBI files, and accessed DMV records. We knew that Jimmy Rantor was the body found on the pier.

However, the investigation was tabled because David's case took precedence. I found some interesting facts. Did you know that Jimmy was arrested in Somerset, Missouri? He was detained for distributing ZTE to the local kids?"

"Yes, it landed him in Juvie."

"The Doctor assigned to do his psychiatric evaluation was Doctor Leslie Ross. She was doing her thesis at Columbia on the effects of the drug Zeta on Human behavior. She wrote that using hypnosis therapy and pharmaceuticals could be an effective treatment for behavioral disorders, such as (get this) Cognitive Dissociative Disorder! Isn't that what you said that Cassy was being treated for?"

"It is."

"I thought so. So, I dug deeper into Doctor Ross' background. An FBI report said that she was reported to the Board of Psychologists for the unauthorized use of human test subjects in her research. During that time, the use of ZETA among street kids and club-goers had declined to almost non-existent. She wanted to take the credit for it by holding a press conference. However, a rainstorm prevented the conference from taking place, and no further information was heard of it. She moved to Chicago and has been in charge of the third floor of the Mercy Hospital's psych ward ever since."

"Great work!"

"Thanks. Does that make Leslie a suspect as well?"

"Not necessarily, but it does make her a person of interest. Do me a favor. Keep this "under your hat" until I figure out where this puzzle piece fits."

"Will do, Boss."

"Also, Jerry found out that forensics has been able to extrapolate more information from the SIM card about Other Brother. Most of their website is encrypted. Whoever developed their web presence didn't want anyone to find it."

"Of course, they wouldn't want you to find it—unless you were a 'friend of the cause.' Keep going, Sharon. You're doing great! I have to go now. I am buying coffee."

"Coffee?" Sharon started to say something, but Dwight had already ended the call.

Holding two cups of coffee, Dwight turned around. Nurse Debbie Sanders stood there with two more cups of coffee and a pensive look. "Whoa! Sorry, I didn't see you standing there."

"I got this for you," she said, handing Dwight one of the cups of coffee. "Cassy is why I started working at Mercy on the third floor."

"She is a rare case," Dwight added. "It wasn't to admire or study her. It was to protect her."

Cassy was patiently waiting for Dwight to return. A shadowy figure stood in the doorway carrying a tray with a small cup of pills and a plastic glass of water filled halfway. "Where's Nurse Debbie?"

"Oh, she transferred to a different department. I am orderly, Kevin. I have your meds here. I have been instructed to make sure that you take them before sunrise. I'll just place them on this little table next to your bed. I will come back for the tray in the morning."

"Thank you."

Dwight and Debbie found a table to sit at. "Protect her from what?"

"Don't get me wrong. Cassy is tough. You can't tell her nothin'. Aside from the CDD, something is amiss about her. Her attitude and behavior are not typical of someone with her condition. At least what I know of her." Her face lost all expression, and her eyes darted around the room. It was almost as if she were afraid of something happening.

"Relax. I am a member of the Chicago Police Force. If anything goes down, I will protect you."

"It will be daylight soon," she says, pulling out a cassette tape from underneath her sleeve. "I risked losing my job to smuggle this out of Leslie's office. You might find it helpful in your investigation. When Leslie has a hypnosis session with a patient, she records it. She records them all and archives them in a safe. It is located on the wall behind a painting. Well, I knew an old friend who occupied that office before Leslie. I also know that she never changed the combo on the safe. She discovered me in her office and fired me, but I didn't leave without this. I managed to slip it into my sleeve and exit the office with it." She looks around. Even empty coffee shops can seem unsafe. She places the tape under his napkin. "It was a tape recorded a long time ago. It's a tape of one of Jimmy's sessions. The one where she discovers a third personality inside of Jimmy. His name is Antonio."

Dwight returned to the hospital room, but it was too late. She had fallen asleep, and Dwight couldn't wake her. The sun was beginning to lighten the sky, meaning Cassy was about to transition into Jimmy. Dwight estimated that he had left with two hours or less. So he sat in the brown recliner in the corner of the room and fell asleep. Cassy's pain had woken her up, and she began to moan. The bandages were soaked with her blood, and her pulse was quickening. She was violently transitioning to her daytime persona—Jimmy Rantor. Dwight had to leave the room to make way for the emergency room staff to put her in a coma and wheel her away to the ICU. Dwight exited the hospital and visited Police headquarters to meet with Sharon and Jerry. The hustle and bustle of headquarters was comforting. After the Other Brother incident with Kyle, everything at the precinct seemed to be getting back to normal. Seeing all the destruction caused by the incident put things in perspective. Dwight was maneuvering his way through the booking desks to the Commissioner's office. It was a large room with a desk and bookshelves in the corner. All of the walls were covered with maps and articles. Most of the collage of images was about the Kinsingsworth case. Held in place with an infrastructure of pushpins, all the facts of the case were displayed on the wall, allowing them to be examined at a glance, patterns to be detected, and persons of interest to be matched with the victims and their locations. Dwight remembers the beginning of the investigation. The evidence board was bare, with only a few clues. It is full now, and anonymous tips are pouring into the office.

Jerry was on the phone when Dwight entered. He motions for Dwight to come in and sit down. Jerry hangs up the phone."Will someone let Miss Kastle know that Detective Hussleman has arrived?" Jerry said with his forefinger on the intercom button. Dwight stood in front of the board. His gaze moved around the board, taking in the visual clues and handwritten facts. Jerry walks in carrying a small piece of paper with notes from his conversation with the person on the phone. "That was National Jewish Hospital. They just received the body of a Debbie Sanders. She was run down in front of the coffee shop across the street from Mercy Hospital. She was coming back from a coffee date with a friend and was struck head-on by oncoming traffic."

"Hey there, Dwight," said a friendly voice from the doorway. It was his super-sleuth...Sharon Kastle. "Hey, Sharon, did you get the thing I requested?"

"Yes, I did. These old tape players are becoming increasingly difficult to find. At least the ones that still function. This one operates on batteries." She sets it down in front of Dwight and presses the play button.

"What you hear is the voice of our illustrious Doctor of Psychology, Leslie Ross. She is Jimmy Rantor's attending physician at Mercy. At the time of this taping, she was not at Mercy Hospital in Chicago. She was an assistant to the Dean of Psychology at Columbia University. Do you know who the Dean of Psychology at Columbia University is?... Guess?" Dwight and Sharon didn't change expression and anticipated the answer, "Aw, c'mon! I was hoping your powers of deductive reasoning would be better than that!"

"Wait! Are you suggesting that Carl Kinsingsworth was a member of Other Brother?"

"Well, the evidence is inconclusive. However, we are decoding more and more of the encrypted SIM card (partially damaged by stomach acids and bile from being swallowed) by the assassin. No, I was going to say that the Dean of Psychology just so happens to be... None other than...Kyle's father—Frank Jacob Templeman."

"Kyle's father! Well, it IS a small world after all!"

"The pieces are starting to fit. We have a troubled teen from Somerset, Missouri. Badly beaten, he enters the Justice system as a minor for a misdemeanor and is offered by the court to have it expunged in exchange for a psychiatric evaluation. He, of course, agrees. He is diagnosed with severe Cognitive Dissociative

Disorder. His treatment is meds and therapy. He improves, but instead of continuing therapy, he decides to escape custody and break his parole. He moves to Chicago and begins a new life as Casandra Davis to hide his true identity. He is still troubled. He is still dangerous."

"While performing at the Lido, she meets David and Kyle. Maybe it wasn't just a coincidence that they met."

"How close were Kyle and his Father? Depending on the closeness of their bond, Kyle could have been sent to find Jimmy and report his whereabouts to his father. However, he did not intend for his best friend to develop feelings for the target—the beautiful and charming—Casandra Davis."

"This must have been before they issued the 'cease and desist order,' and, reported Leslie Ross to the Missouri Board of Psychology." They listened to more of the tape. She introduces Jimmy and herself and begins the process of putting Jimmy under hypnosis. She then switches the conversation to Casandra. Casandra starts to cry and lament about the relationship that she just ended. They talk about it. Leslie asks her who it was that hurt her. She wouldn't give a name. She just sobbed. On the tape, she speaks to both Casandra and Jimmy. One could say that they have a "Group Discussion" to get acquainted. Apparently, Jimmy and Casandra had never met before this session. Dr. Leslie helped them get acquainted. Jimmy was further split into two—younger Jimmy, who they called "James" (approximately 9 years old), and an older version of Jimmy, who is approximately 22 years old. Casandra was the Star, the Diva, the Queen! She only lived her life at night. Therefore, she and Jimmy didn't speak much to each other. Leslie was highly approving of Miss Davis. Casandra Davis remained inside Jimmy's mind, and she didn't start manifesting a physical presence until she moved to Chicago and worked at the Lido." Now that we have all finally met, I want to make sure that we haven't left anyone out," is there anyone else that wants to join us? Anyone? Now is the time to come forward and be seen," said the gentle voice from the tape player.

"There is someone else here," said little James. "James! Shut up! He doesn't want anyone to know he is here."

"He who?"

"His name is Antonio. He is Jimmy's bestie," James added."He's mad at you," Jimmy told Leslie, "He doesn't want to work for you. Yet you keep making him do things. Bad things. He is MY best friend—not yours. You say if he does these things to people, the lightning will go away. The lightning doesn't go away! It never does!" Jimmy's voice starts to get agitated. Leslie is describing David's body as he transitions into Antonio. "Lightning is the trigger. I give Jimmy a dose of Zeta Max during a lightning storm, and he will do whatever I want. Even kill—if that's what I command. He is tortured by the lightning until after the assassination is carried out to its completion." Said a very confident Leslie Ross. She mentioned that these findings are recorded, and the results will be returned to Marcus at the lab."To capture Antonio, we need to force Him out of hiding and show himself," Dwight said. "The answer might be to trigger Jimmy."

"How? We can't just enter Jimmy's mind and unlock a door that doesn't exist."

"I am meeting with Casandra again today. She might have some insight into how to get Antonio to come out of his room."

"I'm curious about the relationship that Casandra was crying about. It would have been after Trevor Whitney attacked her and before David and Kyle. Who was she seeing at that time?" Her answer was standing in the room –right next to her. Realizing her epiphany could get Dwight kicked off the case, and she didn't pursue that tangent. "Whoever it is, it shook her up pretty bad. Bad enough to create an evil persona to carry out these horrific crimes," said Jerry. Sharon glanced at Dwight in judgment. Dwight looked back in defiance of her judgmental stare.

"If there were only a way to get hold of some Zeta," Dwight mused. He was fixated on a plan to flush Antonio out in the open. "Dwight, be careful! Antonio is a trained assassin—trained by Other Brother to carry out cold-blooded MURDER! You are risking your life just to be in the same room with Antonio," Sharon warned. Dwight won't listen and will put himself in harm's way, "I know that you don't think that your feelings for Miss Davis are compromising your judgment, but what if they are?"

"I know what you're saying, Sharon. I am asking you to trust me! Don't worry about me! What I need you to do is gather as much information as possible about Zeta Max. Who manufactures it? What are its ingredients? What are its common uses (if any)? Can you do that?"

"What do you want me to do?" Jerry Mack said; ready for action!

"Find Kyle!" Dwight said, leaving the Evidence Room.

# Chapter Twelve-Ladies and Gentlemen, Antonio!

There is a rustling of plastic bags from a nearby restaurant. They weren't heavy, but the filth from the dumpster had fused some of the bags together. Little Jimmy could hear them running away and laughing. Some could be heard jumping up and hitting the bottom of the street sign in this tiny, unforgiving, Midwestern town. Somerset was poor and rural. Two things you don't want to attach to yourself in your youth. Some parts of the Midwest are home to some of the most savage young people this country has to offer. One wrong turn on the wrong street at the wrong time could prove fatal. Jimmy lived there—in Somerset.

There was one school. All grades were taught at Somerset Elementary/High School. Little Jimmy was six when he attended Somerset Elementary. He was getting ready to go to Somerset High School. Now fourteen years old, severe weather made walking to school nearly impossible in the Spring. Also, Jimmy had a disability. He was afraid of lightning, which made his trek to school even more daunting. His paralyzing phobia rendered him incapacitated at the first sight of a flash—either real or imagined. People made fun of him for it. He would be in the middle of a project at school, see a flash of lightning or a clap of thunder from an incoming storm, and jump, panicking, to the amusement of his classmates. He would wet himself and have to be excused. Kids would wait until no teachers could be seen to do their worst—the physical kind of harm that people post about on social media. He was sent home many times for his phobia, and this irritated his stepfather—Marvin.

Marvin married Jimmy's mother, but he hated her son. He was a promoter of toxic masculinity, and Jimmy didn't "fit the mold of a man's man." He tried everything, and Jimmy couldn't give up his effeminate demeanor. His androgynous appearance compounded the situation. Frustrated and at his wits' end, Marvin asked Jimmy to do the dishes. Jimmy reached over, put on his mother's flowered apron, and gently tied it around his waist. Her rubber gloves were in the pocket, and he slid them on. His fingers were too short for the gloves, but he thought the gloves would keep the skin on his hands from cracking. Marvin slid up behind Jimmy. Without realizing what he was doing, Marvin kissed Jimmy on the neck. He asked Jimmy what he was doing. Jimmy sheepishly said, "I am doing the dishes like you asked."

Realizing that Jimmy was not his mother, his stepfather jumped back in horror. Angry and drunk, He took the belt off his pants and secured it between Jimmy's bite. Jimmy tried screaming, but the belt was too tight. He was calling for his mom, but she was vacuuming in the hallway and couldn't hear his screams. She cleaned the house with earbuds piping in her favorite tunes. Martha was transported to "Music Land" in the trailer, oblivious to her surroundings. Struggling to breathe so that he could get free, Marvin had him pinned to the floor and kept tightening the belt around his mouth like a horse bridle. His mother heard the noise and started screaming at Jimmy. She kept asking him over and over, "What did you do? Jimmy, why are you doing this?" He couldn't respond to her, and Marvin wasn't about to put a hold on his rage. He had no clue that the fire of his abuse would unleash a demon— Marvin inadvertently created the Black Widow's Ghost. Jimmy was turning red. Marvin picked him up by the neck and, with his belt still squeezing his mouth, dragged Jimmy outside. When Jimmy tried to stand, Marvin would yank on the belt. Jimmy fell back down to the ground. It broke Jimmy's lower jaw. He was screaming at Jimmy that the front yard was where he would live from now on. With one grunt, he hurled Jimmy off the front porch of the chocolate brown and white trailer. The "thud" was so loud that it should have awakened the neighbors. All the neighbors' porch lights were on, but no one came outside. Marvin's breath wreaked of Kentucky Gold Whiskey. Jimmy broke. He could no longer move his mouth. His face was cut up and bloody. This might be his last night on earth.

Still struggling to breathe and pulling at the restraint around his face, Jimmy started to urinate. The warm liquid running down his leg frightened him, and he began flailing about. His eyes filled with desperation. His saliva made the leather slide around his mouth, allowing the belt to cut through his skin. The mixture produced pink and red marble droplets dripping from Jimmy's mouth. Marvin was cutting his face open. Marvin had him on the ground and was watching him die. Jimmie's mother stood on the front porch and preached, "This is what happens if you don't change your ways." Marvin had his knees embedded in Jimmy's chest and was putting all of his weight on Jimmy's sternum. Jimmy was gasping and turning blue, and his eyes rolled back."OH NO, YOU DON'T! I'M NOT THROUGH WITH YOU YET!!" Marvin picked Jimmy up and pulled the belt off Jimmy's broken and bleeding jaw. Jimmy took one breath, and WHAM! Marvin had balled up his fist and gave Jimmy a right cross to the face. Shattering his occipital lobe and breaking Jimmy's nose. The blood squirted onto Marvin's face, and his hands were soaked in blood as he kept hitting Jimmy over and over. Jimmy was off the ground and pinned to a tree, and all he could do was kick. He kept straightening his feet to try to feel how high off the ground he was. Both of his eyes were swollen shut. He couldn't feel the punches or touch the ground anymore. His lower jaw was hanging and unresponsive. Then Marvin went for the ribs. In his mind, Marvin was ridding the world of Evil, not creating it. One less "freak will make the world ,at least his world, a better place. From the throw off the porch, Jimmy was already bruised. With every punch, he could feel his ribs crack. His body went limp, and he closed his eyes. Around the corner, a tall, handsome, Italian-looking man who also lived in the same park in Somerset came flying through the grassy pathway with his hands holding a baseball bat and a cold, determined hero's look in his eye. He saw Jimmy against the tree. A rope around his neck. He saw Marvin manning the other end of the rope. He saw Jimmy move his finger. Antonio saw that Jimmy was hanging on for dear life. With one toss over the lowest branch, the rope was set. Marvin was ready to hoist Jimmy's lifeless corpse into the air.

Antonio dealt one crack to the knees, and Marvin hit the ground. He hit him again in the head and knocked Marvin out. Then he just kept hitting him until he wasn't moving anymore. He loosened the rope around Jimmy's neck. Jimmy's mother had called the police. She was in her bathrobe, on the phone, describing the scene to law enforcement. He didn't know if he had committed murder or not, but he didn't want to stick around and find out. In case this assault turns into a homicide, he had better get Jimmy and get the hell out of there. He was able to get Jimmy's body out of the tree and get him to a safe area in the trailer park. Antonio was homeless and stayed with a lady whom he called "Mama." He brought Jimmy to Mama's house. He dressed his wounds and let Jimmy rest until morning. After a few encouraging words from "Mama," they took Jimmy to the hospital. He had to have some reconstruction, but overall, he pulled through, thanks to Antonio.

Antonio and Jimmy became inseparable friends. They hung out on the streets of Somerset. They committed petty crimes and antagonized the police. Jimmy helped Antonio take care of "Mama." She had diabetes and was always in pain. When she had "bad days," they would help with household chores and run errands. That summer, Jimmy healed enough to attend high school in the fall. Over the summer, Antonio taught Jimmy how to fight on the streets. Jimmy would no longer be a victim. Jimmy was quiet and quick. He would use that to do justice to those who sought to cause him harm.

Now, months later, Jimmy was walking home from school, and three high school seniors jumped him, beat him up, and threw him in a dumpster. Left to his fate, Jimmy recalled his home life and all of his step-dads. Those brutal memories became his demon friends, and the soul of the young man began to turn. He was broken, and healing him this time would take a miracle. Like shattered glass, even if he could find a way to piece back together his broken soul, the cracks in the glass would keep a true reflection from showing. So, he vowed never to look into another mirror for as long as he lived. He lifted himself out of the dumpster and chased after those three boys. Jimmy felt the spirit of his friend, Antonio, pour through him as he exacted his revenge on those three boys. One of them had a fractured thumb and forefinger, another one had a bloody ear, and the third got scared and ran off. The reward was bittersweet, and Jimmy attributed his newfound courage to his friend, Antonio, and the teachings he had shared.

Antonio met up with Jimmy later, and Jimmy told him the story. They shared a laugh. The night that Jimmy lost his virginity was to Antonio. They were bros, and their bond was forged in fire. So, when Jimmy confessed to Antonio that he had never been with anyone in a sexual way, Antonio took pity on his friend. They shared a night together, and Jimmy's love for his friend grew stronger. He had never thought that he could love anyone. The pain inflicted on him kept him from feeling such intimate feelings. Antonio was the closest thing to love that Jimmy had ever experienced. Jimmy would do anything for him. Anything...even kill if need be. That one night led to the next two weeks of good feelings, exploration, and adventure. Sometimes, they would sit around the house and talk about nothing. They would scheme and plot against people they didn't like. They made plans to leave Somerset and create a life together in a City where no one would judge them for who they were. Jimmy mentioned that he wanted to live in New York City. He felt that even the roughest parts of the "Big Apple" had promise. When they weren't having sex, they were causing trouble. Just about that time, a new party drug had entered their small town. A drifter hanging out in front of the grocery store in their area gave them a small zipper bag. Inside the bag were two blue pills. He called it Zeta. They bought it and went back to Mama's house to try it. The drug gave them a euphoria like that of Marijuana, but it lasted six to eight hours. The effects started to diminish. Afterward, they became super-energetic and agitated. Another 45 minutes, and they would "crash and burn." They slept for two days. It became a fun thing to do on the weekends. Jimmy always tried to keep it on him so that he could do it with Antonio or sell it for cash to the other kids at school. Antonio got caught. Mama got a call from the police department. Antonio had been taken into custody, and they were getting ready to book him. At his hearing, the judge offered him the choice of either three years in prison or serving in the military. He had no other choices. All of his options had been exhausted. Antonio took the deal. He left for the Marines right from the detention center.

Jimmy never saw him. Never said goodbye. Never got closure. He doesn't know where Antonio went or if he will ever see his dear Antonio again. Jimmy experienced his first pain of a lost love. Despair and hopelessness can run as deep as the ocean and manifest themselves in physical ways. People are as rare and precious as diamonds. No two are ever the same. The flaws and imperfections are what give diamonds their value. Jimmy clung to that analogy, though his evaluation of his situation made finding diamonds impossible. Whether it be people or gemstones, the precious ones remained elusive. Nothing illuminates diamonds like lightning, which is the one thing he needed to enjoy maximum sparkle—should he ever encounter these rare beauties. He knew they were out there. He just needed to know where to look. Precious gems can even be found under rocks when you pick them up to see what is underneath. Even in the rain, the lightning can show where they are. Even when hiding inside a rock, lightning can strike it, and the rock cracks open to reveal the diamond in the rough. Jimmy realized that lightning was the catalyst for finding the precious diamonds. But once he discovered them, how would he show them off? A bracelet? Perhaps a pinky ring?" That just won't do," Jimmy thought, "It must be ...A NECKLACE!"

Antonio was the most precious thing to Jimmy. Whenever it rained, Jimmy no longer panicked at the flashes of lightning in the sky. Antonio not only cured him of his phobia, but now, he appears to Jimmy in his dreams. Horrifying dreams of blood and killing in gruesomely creative ways. Jimmy was searching for Antonio, his precious friend. Jimmy's obsession turned to madness. Since he was no longer afraid, he felt unstoppable. No one could touch him or Antonio. Antonio was a part of him now. Together, they would conquer the world.

Thus, Antonio was born. Jimmy felt as if a part of him had been fulfilled. He would now carry on as a normal person. Lightning still bothered him, but it didn't paralyze him. Jimmy now had a purpose. He wanted Diamonds. As many as he could get. He would collect them. However, he could only get the sparkling jewels in a pawn shop in Somerset. "Somerset Pawn Shop" was the place to go if you needed quick cash. Anyone could buy, sell, or trade anything. The manager there was none other than the old woman Antonio used to care for. She had no idea why Antonio left and was heartbroken. Jimmy would occasionally drop off a bag of Zeta for her. They would get high together and talk about Antonio and Diamonds. She was losing sight, and after a few months, she started calling out to Antonio. Jimmy now answered her as Antonio. He adjusted his voice and speech pattern to mimic the missing Marine. He practiced in the mirror. Changing his appearance to match old photos of Antonio. He practiced every subtlety until the lines between Jimmy and Antonio were blurred. Jimmy was convinced that he had created his version of Antonio. His friend was always with him, always by his side, and ready to do what Jimmy could not— eliminate anyone who got in his way. Jimmy now had a different view of his life and people. He no longer felt the bottomless despair. If he did, Antonio would help him feel better. Antonio was better at talking to people. And he could kill with no remorse. This frightened Jimmy. This inner conflict manifested in ways that made Jimmy appear insane, and he asked Antonio not to involve him in it anymore. To an ordinary observer, Jimmy, as a young man talking to himself, is only Jimmy resolving a conflict with Antonio. Antonio gets frustrated and goes to a place in Jimmy's mind where no one can go, not even Jimmy himself. Antonio closed the door and locked it behind him. He only came out when Jimmy needed him.

Jimmy locked him away, but he always kept the key nearby when he needed to summon Antonio quickly.

In the past, Jimmy summoned Antonio to show him the makeup techniques he had learned online. The idea was to enhance Antonio's appearance. Jimmy studied them and practiced on himself. Then, Jimmy taught these techniques to Antonio. By now, Jimmy could completely transform and look nothing like his former self. Experimentation leads to creativity—he would call this the creative side of him... Casandra Davis. Yes, the three lived rent-free inside Jimmy's head. They were all separate but exchanged ideas, strategies, recipes, quips, and anecdotes. It was entertaining to watch from afar, but dangerous if one got too close. Casandra Davis didn't understand why she wasn't allowed the same freedom that some of the "others" enjoyed. She constantly threw tantrums and caused considerable chaos. She frequently fought with Jimmy and Antonio. Antonio disappeared for a while after Jimmy escaped from the "Facility," moved to Chicago, and joined the cast of performers at The Lido. He went into hiding...

Antonio was a sleeping giant who only needed to be awakened. Clouds were forming, and the barometric pressure was high.

# Chapter Thirteen-The Zeta Sun Always Sets in Cancun

Sharon walks into the forensics lab to speak to her old friend, Lillie Baxter. Lillie and Sharon studied criminology together at Illinois State University. Their years in college brought them closer. When graduation day arrived, they both secured jobs with the Chicago Police Department. Lillie went into forensics and became the top expert in her field, while Sharon pursued a career in detective work. They were both working with the cybersecurity department. Their ultimate goal? To break through the encrypted files on Other Brother website. The process was tedious and slow. So, to find David's and the Mayor's assassins, they were in a race against time.

It had been raining all week, and Sharon arrived at the lab wet and dripping. She walked through the electronic double doors with dramatic flair. Each step seemed to be illuminated by a FLASH of lightning and a CRACK of thunder. She made her way to the second floor. It was closed for the evening, so there was no one around. Eerily quiet, she couldn't detect any janitors or security guards roaming the hallway. Strange to her, it seemed as if the power had been temporarily knocked out. The message on her phone was just as cryptic and weird, "I've got it! You're gonna want to see this!" So, Sharon wasted no time getting to the lab. Now that she had finally arrived, her pace was slower and more cautious as she moved toward the lab ahead of her. The lightning illuminated the long hallway to the lab. With each flash, she could quicken her step—knowing that there didn't seem to be any objects or people in her way. The door to the lab had been breached. The glass was broken and littered on the ground. She walked in, but the lab was empty. Sharon drew her sidearm and proceeded into the room. The emergency lights came on, flickering periodically from the storm taxing the city's electrical grid. This startled her, but she made it quietly to the computer. The chair in front of the computer was empty. The screensaver was on. Sharon positioned the keyboard in front of the screen and clicked the mouse to pull up the menu. Nothing happened. The screensaver went away to reveal a prompt for the password. Lillie obviously broke through the encryption. Weeks of hard work paid off, but she could only get to the password prompt. The complex website was difficult to breach. Lillie's message likely pertained to what she discovered after crossing the firewall. Where would she have put the password? "Whoever built this site does NOT want us in here!" She mused. Trying random passwords might shut down the system and cause it to automatically change or alter the password process. What Sharon needed was a clue. Why did Lillie send her a text message and not show up for their meeting? Sharon began searching the room for anything that might reveal an answer. Then she saw, in her peripheral vision, a grey locker that said "BAXTER" on it. This was Lillie's locker. She walked up to it, looked down at her feet, and noticed a roof leak. Water was dripping from the ceiling. It had pooled on the floor directly in front of the locker. She looked up at the ceiling to find the source of the leak, but the ceiling tiles appeared dry. She stood still and didn't see or hear any dripping water. She held out her hand to try to capture a falling raindrop. Nothing happened. She wasn't able to find out anything else in the dark. There was no sign of Lillie. Sharon decided to return and speak with Lillie in the morning during working hours. Just then, she heard movement in the locker. She jumped, but carefully, and she tried to control her surprise. When she realized the implications of the noise from the locker, she realized her throat was dry. She tried to swallow. Sharon slowly placed her sidearm back in the holster but left it unsnapped. Apprehension gripped her. She denied what her instincts were screaming at her. She gingerly placed one hand on the latch and, with one motion, unlatched the door and opened it. Inside the cold metal locker was a battered and weakened Lillie, barely breathing and clinging to life. She was dying, and there was little Sharon could do. If she attempts to call emergency responders, they will arrive too late. The only option for Sharon was to hold Lillie, tell her how much she was loved, and apologize for not spending more time with her friend. Lillie started gasping and aspirating blood from her sliced trachea. Sharon was applying pressure, but Lillie was losing too much blood. In one last effort before her passing, Lillie looked up at Sharon and raised her arm to the door. It was a picture of their day at the beach. They were smiling and standing outside, in front of the ocean, wearing giant sun hats and a white triangle of zinc oxide on their noses. Sharon started to cry for her friend. So beautiful. She was so smart. She did not deserve this as her fate. Sharon was soaked in Lillie's blood. Lillie was unable to hold her arm up any longer. She flopped her arm to the side and began fading away. Sharon took the photo from the locker and placed it lovingly in Lillie's hand. With that, Lillie took one last breath and said goodbye—forever at peace.

Sharon could not control the waves of grief flooding her body. She didn't want her friend to be part of this body count. She screamed out in agony and rocked her lifeless body to rest. There was movement in the corridor. Sharon gently placed her friend back in the locker and drew her sidearm again. She entered the hallway with extreme caution. She walked over the broken glass and crept into the hallway. Her gun pointed in the direction of her gaze. Emergency power illuminated specific areas while the rest of the lab remained cloaked in shadow. A crack of lightning revealed a dark figure at the end of the hallway. It glanced back at Sharon and then bolted out of the building. She couldn't make out a face or any other detail. They were there, then they vanished into the storm. Sharon called for backup. Officers were on their way. The time is 2:16 am.

Dwight was back at the Hospital. He was in the pharmaceutical department doing a little snooping. He was using their database to try to locate Zeta Max. He was unable to find anything. He searched the internet. He found articles on Zeta but not Zeta Max. Dwight's gut told him the only way to find Zeta Max was to crack the encryption code on the Other Brother website. Dwight was sure the information was there. Nothing was on the shelves. There was a safe against the far wall. "Why would there be a safe against the wall?" Dwight asked himself. His conclusion was that it possessed the "highly-secured" drugs—drugs that they didn't want to fall into the wrong hands. He imagined opiates, hallucinogens, and expensive, hard-to-get drugs. He read about a drug for the treatment of brain tumors that was $25,000.00 for one dose. If the Hospital had Zeta Max, it also would've been kept in the safe. Dwight returned to Cassy's room because he was unable to access the safe or its contents. Dwight could find out what pharmaceuticals the Hospital was giving to Cassy. Anything other than painkillers, she may not be aware of. Perhaps Jimmy knows the medications Cassy has been taking. There was Miss Davis in full regalia. She wore makeup and had managed to tear a piece of a bed sheet into a thin belt to tie around her waist. Finally, her hospital gown began to take on a more shapely likeness of a dress. She looks at Dwight and asks him what he thinks. He just flashes a masculine semi-grin and takes her hand. He pulls her in close. She noticed that his mood had changed. She noticed that his gaze was altered somehow. He maintains expression. Dwight looks into her eyes. He is searching for something inside of her. Something she may not even know about herself. Antonio was locked away inside her somewhere. Miss Davis was afraid to show him "The Room."

"I have to go," Dwight said, still holding Miss Davis in his arms.

"Where are you going?" She gives him a sardonic look, "Have I displeased you?" Miss Davis gives a laugh to get a reaction. Dwight leans in. He kisses her.

"The sun will be coming up soon," he said. He gently kisses her again. His hands start to trace the curve of her hip. She slyly reaches around and gets a handful of Dwight's "Linebacker cheeks." His kiss goes deep. She closes her eyes and notices that the detective has a rise in his business casual slacks. He presses against her.

"How long has it been?" She whispers softly in his left ear.

"Not too long, I am married, you know."

"How's that working out for you?" She reached for the back of his head. She runs her fingers through his thick, manly forest of coarse, chestnut-brown hair. He is strong and confident. And now, he is putty in her hands. "Do you have any Zeta?" Dwight asked her. His tone sounded like he was asking for himself. It was lighthearted and flirtatious. "What do you know about it? Zeta?" She laughed at him. "What! They don't make it anymore? C'mon!... Let's get some!"

"I haven't spoken to my 'Guy' in a while. I wouldn't know where (or how) to get it." Dwight pulls away.

"I can make a few calls? Try to score some? I know you, Dwight. You don't need Zeta. No one does."

"So, what about painkillers?"

"What about them?"

"Give me one. I bet you've got some good painkillers here. Opiates? Hydro's? What have you got?"

"Okay, you're creeping me out..."

"Come on, Babe," Dwight grabs her by the waist, pulls her against his big, strong body, and kisses her passionately on the mouth. He feels Casandra go limp in his arms. She is putty.

"All they give me here are these little blue pills to treat my phobia."

"You have a phobia? What is it?"

"Dwight, you know I have a fear of lightning." Yes, Dwight was aware of her phobia. She still had the crippling fear of lightning that she had when they dated.

"Next time, save one for me," Dwight said. He kisses her on the lips one last time and squeezes her perfectly shaped breast. She returns the favor and sends him off with an erection that causes him to walk funny. She smiles, watches him walk to the hallway, and immediately collapses. Cassy hollers for the attending male nurse before she falls on the floor. Without any hesitation, he sees her on the floor, holding her abdomen. Her gown is stained red. Just then, the sun began to turn the sky a light blue. Her heart monitor beats more rapidly, and the alarm sounds a code blue. The nurses remove her makeup and wig. The gurney comes into the room, And they transfer the patient to the I.C.U. Within minutes, she is transported, the hemorrhaging is stopped, and Jimmy is placed in a medically induced coma.

Dwight heads down to the station, where Sharon and Jerry Mack continue piecing together more clues. In the evidence room, the photograph of Lillie Baxter—Sharon's long-time friend and fellow alumnus- was added to the forensic photos of the injuries that caused her passing. A somber Sharon Kastle stood in front of the board. Her posture was slouched, and her head bowed in reflection. Her arms were crossed, and one hand was covering her mouth like a barrier to keep her feelings from escaping her lips. She was freshly showered, and her hair was blown dry. She was wearing a little makeup to hide the sorrowful puffiness of her mourning. Dwight sauntered up beside her. Silent, at first. The long pause was too dramatic for him, so Dwight broke the silence.

"This is personal now. Lillie was my good friend. She didn't deserve this," Sharon's eyes began to overflow with emotion." She served the people. She deserved a long life and to die with dignity, in a warm bed, surrounded by friends and family." Tears were starting to stream down, ruining her makeup. Dwight reached over and gave his partner a hug. The hug that only a handsome man with strength and determination could provide. He looks at the mascara running down her face. Images of David's body with makeup streaming in the rain crept into Dwight's mind. Their moment was short-lived. However, Sharon's desire for revenge lit a fire that became a rite of passage from rookie to seasoned.

"Don't worry, Sharon, we will find her killer and avenge your good friend's death."

"Thanks, Dwight."

"Have you seen Jerry?"

"He's at the Coffee Station. Getting coffee."

"I asked Casandra if she had any access to Zeta."

"It's Zeta Max." Sharon corrected.

"I know. Something tells me that Zeta Max is not on the open market. Therefore, Cassy would have no knowledge of it (and would therefore be unwilling to talk about it anyway). She did tell me about the medication that they are giving her to help treat her lightning phobia. It's a little blue pill."

"I can have her hospital records subpoenaed," Jerry Mack said, entering the room and handing Sharon a round of coffee. "It's only a matter of time before Other Brother gets wind of what we're doing, which puts Miss Davis in danger. She is our only witness to what happened to David."

"I can have it on my desk in an hour. Meanwhile, our cybersecurity division has hit a roadblock. Every time they enter a password, the system shuts down and becomes re-encrypted. It's been 7 hours, and they still can't get through."

"Moments before her passing, Lillie tried to grasp hold of this picture." Sharon unfolds her right arm and points to the photo of her and Lillie in Cancun, "Before she could say anything, she took her last breath...and she was gone."

"Forensics examined the picture. There were no fingerprints. There was no DNA. On the front or back of the picture," Jerry said, "Just the words CANCUN 2025 in red ink on the back."

"Wait! That picture wasn't taken in Cancun," Sharon said as her eyes widened, "It was taken in Cabo San Lucas—in 2005!"

In Dwight's mind, he was starting to "work out the math." The photograph was a clue. Lillie was trying to convey a message to Sharon just before her passing. When she messaged Sharon, Lillie cracked the encryption to the Other Brother website. Dwight's instinct suggested that she might have discovered the password and gained access to the site. Once inside, Lillie had found something. A clue that could blow this case wide open. What was it?

"Go down to the lab," Dwight says, removing the picture from the evidence wall and handing it to Sharon. "Have them do a DNA test on the red ink."

"You think it's Blood?" Sharon was going over the implications in her mind. If it was Lillie's blood, she might have found the password and could have written it on the back of the photo. "I do. Either Lillie's blood or the blood of her killer. I think that it's a message. Lillie wasn't trying to hang on to some college memory. She was trying to point to the message on the back of this photo—

written in her blood. Although I would rather have all of this be confirmed with the lab's DNA test."

"Well, what are we waiting for!! We have a real lead! LET'S MOVE PEOPLE!" It was only another one of Dwight's hunches. This one felt so strong that Dwight was willing to test the password on the encrypted website, risking the systemic shutdown and resetting of the encryption, and destroying all of the cybersecurity team's efforts to break into the Other Brother website. Dwight bolted for the lab. Sharon ran to the forensic lab and demanded that they stop everything they were doing and run a DNA test on the photo in her hand. She was not willing to risk the disappearance of this all-important piece of evidence, so she didn't hand it off to anyone. She stayed and recorded the whole process on her phone. Sharon also interviewed each member of the forensics team and recorded each interview. Jerry Mack called the DA's office and apologized for contacting them at such a late hour. He asked the District Attorney to order a subpoena of Jimmy Rantor's medical records to be entered into the "David Kinsingsworth Murder Case" as evidence. Dwight went to the Cybersecurity office and gently closed the door to one of the back offices. Everyone had gone home for the evening. Alone and armed with the words Cancun 2025. He sat down and started typing the password. The website was encrypted. He ran the decoding software, and within approximately 25 minutes, Dwight generated the password prompt. He typed the words exactly as he remembered seeing them on the back of Lillie's college photograph, "CANCUN 2025." Nothing. Undaunted, Dwight had two more tries. He typed in "Cancun 2025." Immediately, the opening page to Other Brother loaded onto the screen. "Welcome. Let us introduce ourselves..." This introductory page introduced the reader to the organization, Other Brother, and what it stands for. There were other areas on the website. But one in particular had our detective intrigued. It was a blank drop-down menu. There was nothing on it. It just dropped down. Instead of listing what items are in that particular area of the website. It was totally blank.

Dwight played with the drop-down menu for a little while. He discovered that he was able to type in it. It was a search bar hidden in the menu. So, he typed in "Z," and the letters "Z.M." appeared. He clicked on the initials, and an article came up. It was a memo outlining the persuasive properties of certain mind-altering substances and how they can be used to get citizens to obey commands—even without their being conscious. It further went on to discuss the street drug Zoro Tropo Entropine. It gave the recipe for making the street version of the drug. Dwight kept reading. It said, "For more information on the effects of Zeta on the human brain—see the Leslie Ross files. The hair on Dwight's neck began to tingle and stand up. He had been confiding in Cassy's therapist this whole time. All the while, Leslie could have been conspiring to turn Jimmy Rantor into a cold-blooded killer. She was a member of Other Brother and worked to create a more sinister version of Zeta. She was using Jimmy as a guinea pig. So, in the same search menu, Dwight typed in "Leslie Ross Tapes," and many options populated the dialog box. He began reading at the top and continued. Dr. Ross' research was extensive. Her article on the effects of Zeta on the human mind was impeccable. Her recordings of the hypnosis sessions with Jimmy were enlightening but sometimes heartbreaking. The amount of abuse this man suffered was staggering to the young detective. Jimmy never had the love and support that a 'normal' child usually takes for granted in a loving, supportive household. To be honest, Dwight admitted that he didn't have an easy childhood, but what this little boy had to endure was relentless, methodical, and unforgiving. The things that Jimmy had to recall under hypnosis were hard to hear with all of the raw emotions of a 9-year-old boy. Dwight could not listen to those parts, so he skipped them and moved on to the next set of recordings.

Each session was a progressive therapy that eventually altered the mental state of this already unstable person. Dr. Leslie Ross created within Jimmy an entity so cold and calculating that by the time she was finished Jimmy's conditioning, he could commit lethal crimes for money without remorse, deposit the funds the next day, and carry on as if it was his job—because cold-blooded killing was his actual job. People aren't humanly capable of committing such heinous crimes every day. Jimmy was no exception. The others did not approve of Antonio's "upgrades" and often they aired their differences to Dr. Leslie. All of them wanted it to stop. It was hurting them and destroying Antonio. Leslie used the phobia of lightning to keep a "tight hold" on the assassin she created. She made Antonio believe that if he carried out these orders, assassinating various enemies of Other Brother, it would cure his lightning phobia. The doses of Zeta Max allowed him to carry out the tasks with impunity—often having a vague or no memory of the target's elimination. It gave him the illusion that killing cured his phobia. However, the reality was that the relief was only temporary—much to Antonio's despair.

On the Other Brother website, the chemical ingredients of Zeta Max were listed, along with instructions on how to make it. Dwight took a pic of the screen with the recipe. He headed back to the lab to see if they could recreate it. Sharon was there. Awaiting the result of the DNA test on the photo. Dwight walked in, and the technician entered the room to deliver his findings. The file was tightly tucked under the lab tech's armpit as he walked to the two detectives.

"It worked. I was able to get into the Other Brother website," Dwight whispered in Sharon's ear. "Great Job! This is the technician in charge of getting the test results. I think he's ready."

"Well, it is blood. It's Lillie's Blood." With the results revealed, the two detectives went back. They scoured the Other Brother website for everything they could on the assassination of David, his father, Debbie, the nurse, Lillie, the forensic pathologist, and whoever else. In fact, Other Brother has a complete list of possible threats to them and their ideologies. With a strong willingness to quiet, these would be "distractions" from their ultimate destiny—the cleansing of society to make way for a superior new race of human beings. With enough evidence to catch Other Brother, Dwight thought about what would happen to Casandra if Other Brother decided that she was more of a liability than an asset. To be able to do this to a human—so thoroughly, disregarding the health or well-being of Jimmy Rantor, they wouldn't have any problem putting an end to the "Black Widow's Ghost." Jimmy was an eyewitness, evidence, and needed to be protected. As long as he was in the Hospital, under the watchful eye of Dr. Leslie, he was vulnerable. He had to be taken somewhere safe. Somewhere away from Dr. Leslie and the watchful eye of Other Brother.

The sun was going down. Jimmy's transformation began. Dwight had to get back and talk to Casandra about sneaking out of the Hospital. Sharon and the district attorney began copying files from the Other Brother's website. They were racing against the clock, issuing search warrants, arrest warrants, and subpoenas, and started building their case. The lab was able to create several doses of Zeta Max according to the recipe screenshot that Dwight delivered to them. Sharon had secured all the evidence. It was in a secret place where it could not be tampered with or erased. Jerry Mack called in a special SWAT team and FBI agents to help bring in for questioning, Other Brother Members are listed on the website. There were 73 names on that list. The names targeted for elimination were notified about their situation and instructed to remain on high alert until the investigation was completed. Dwight took three doses of Zeta Max in a vile and closed the lid. He shoved them in his pocket, and just as the sun descended on the horizon, Dwight made his way to Mercy. With the pieces in place, it was time to take down Antonio—the Black Widow's Ghost, and let justice decide how this chapter will "play out."

# Chapter Fourteen-Birth of a Ghost

There is an argument in the office of the Dean of Psychiatry. It is May 2012. The voices that can be heard are those of Dean Franklin Jacob Templeman and Mayor Carl Kinsingsworth. They are arguing about the newly appointed assistant to Dean Templeman—Leslie Ross. Carl was upset because of some of the studies that were being done to ascertain the effects of the party drug ZETA on the human mind. Human trials of variants and combinations of hypnosis were being used on actual human test subjects. Prisoners and illegal immigrants were among the human guinea pigs.

"I have done everything I can to get this drug ZTE off the streets, and you want to continue to manufacture it? This is outrageous! And what about this student—Leslie? You are forcing her to do this against her will. She could threaten to expose us, the organization; it all feels like it's falling apart, Frank! I want out! I have my career to think about...and I am taking Leslie with me."

"It's not that easy, Carl. You can't just opt out! In its current state, ZTE is of no use to us. Take it off the streets—that's fine. I have developed a formula using the root form of ZETA (ZTE), but made it more useful for the organization's purposes. It takes away a subject's inhibitions and allows an individual to obey commands without impunity!" Said Dean Templeman with passion and conviction in his voice. "The raw ingredients can be traced back to O.B.—to us! I don't care what you do. I just don't want any part of it!"

"We don't want you to do anything that's against your code of ethics. Just help us by keeping the FBI off our trail."

"I am saying I want out! It was fine in College, but things like secret societies and radical ideologies have no place in the lives of intelligent adults. This is the real world, Frank. We all need to quit this childhood nonsense and grow the hell up!"

"Other Brother is expanding, and soon, it will infiltrate the lives of almost everyone on the planet. There will be no escape. We will find you! Align with us, or we will have no choice but to..."

"TO WHAT?" Carl looked Frank straight in the face. Eye to eye, Carl slowly turned around and exited the room.

Leslie Ross is in a hospital room with a battered and bruised Jimmy Rantor. He is 14 years old.  The lights are dimmed so that Jimmy doesn't feel triggered in any way. She is holding him and rocking him back and forth. He looks up at her.


"I have known you for a very long time. Haven't I? Why are you so nice to me?"

"Jimmy, I have something to tell you. When I first saw you, Jimmy, you were 9 years old. You were so badly hurt. The medical team and I didn't know if you would make it. The doctors healed you, and I treated you for the trauma. I have treated you on and off for years and kept track of your whereabouts. When I found out that they were going to send you to juvie, I made them release you to my custody instead. I have taken an interest in you because I am your real mother, Jimmy. Martha Rantor is your adopted mother. You were genetically created from my egg and Dean Templeman's sperm. I carried you to term. After you were born, we allowed Martha and Marvin to adopt you. They lived close enough away so that we could monitor your growth. The attempt on your life was unexpected. Placing you in the ghost program was unintentional, but you displayed abilities that the other subjects didn't have and wouldn't be able to acquire. So, we continued to train you. We treated your injuries and your trauma and sent you home."

"I didn't go home."

"We know Jimmy. You hush now; there's no need to relive the past."

"Did you not like Cassy's boyfriend, David? Why did you want Antonio to hurt him?"

"He was on the list."

"I don't like the list."

"If you don't take care of the list, you will get struck by lightning. It will hunt you down and strike you dead. Understand?"

"Yes, Doctor Leslie."

That night, Casandra gets up from her bed and walks to the nurse's station. She is in her hospital gown and a sash tied around her waist. "Where's Leslie? Can I talk to Leslie, please?" Casandra said. She was out of sorts. She had taken her blue pills, and it agitated her. Leslie came out of the hallway with a concerned look on her face and approached the nurse's desk with caution.

"Cassy... What is it? Why aren't you in bed?"

"Is it true? Did you make Antonio kill David? How could you do that? I loved him!"

"Casandra, what are you talking about, my dear? I didn't make anyone do anything.

David and Kyle were sent to find you. When they found out that you were performing at the Lido Downtown, they were going to kidnap you and bring you back to the ' Facility' to finish your training. That didn't work out. Did it?... "

"Antonio told me everything. He's here with me."

"It's the meds, Cassy. Here, let's get you back to bed," Leslie grabs Casandra gently by the arm and starts to walk her back to her room. She helps Casandra get back into bed and covers her legs with the hospital blanket.

"I need to speak to Antonio, please. Right now," Leslie waited for a few seconds. She could tell by the change in expression and the way that her face contorted a certain way that Antonio was present, "Antonio, why would you tell Casandra such things about me? I am your mother!"

"You're Jimmy's mother. You're not my mother." Antonio said, "You're not Cassy's moms either. She never knew you before."

"Antonio, I need you to listen. It's going to storm."

"No, you've got to listen. I don't want to be here. I hate bein' locked up in my room until you tell me it's safe to come out. I told Cassy everything. All of the people that you made me kill, where I learned to fight, all my training, all of it."

"Why did you do that, Antonio? She is not supposed to know Jimmy either."

"CUZ I'M SICK OF IT! THE FEAR NEVER GOES AWAY! YOU HAVE MADE ME KILL ALL THESE PEOPLE, BUT after I do, THE PAIN AND FEAR NEVER GO AWAY! I AM SICK OF IT! THE ONLY THING YOU WANT ME TO DO IS KILL FOR YOU AND HURT PEOPLE FOR YOU! I TRIED TO GET AWAY FROM YOU!

I escaped to Chicago and found Casandra to get away from you! BUT YOU FOUND ME! I JUST WANT TO BE LEFT ALONE!"

"I can make all the fear go away!"

"How?"

"Just one more list and we will all be free to live out our lives without fear. Would you like that? This is the last hit list! I'm serious this time, Jimmy."

"I am ANTONIO!" He grabbed her by the neck and lifted her off the ground. Leslie was frightened and started kicking. Antonio lowered her back to the ground, and she caught her breath. "One more! Here is the number. Once you're finished, the money will be wired to your account," Leslie says, taking out a pen and writing seven digits on Jimmy's arm. "You will want to commit this number to memory because the ink will disappear in 15 minutes. Now take your pills and go change your clothes."

"My bag with the 'face stuff' is in that little closet over there." He points to a small closet against the wall. It had a black duffle bag and a change of clothes in all-black. The bag also contained the cloaking device that enabled Antonio to carry out his task without being detected by security cameras. It is a spray that, when applied to the face and hands, distorts the wearer's appearance. Rendered undetectable to any camera or phone, our assassin appears as nothing more than a shadow on the screen. A small device the size of a belt buckle is attached to Antonio's belt. With several atomized passes over his face and neck, spraying with the special concealer that makes his appearance blurred, Antonio presses a button. The electrical pulse alters the shape and structure of his face, rendering it unrecognizable to anyone who sees him. The spray alone is ineffective. It must be activated. The nanotechnology emits an electronic signal that alerts the microbes in the concealer to create a contrary pattern on Antonio's face within seconds. To the security cameras, he looks like a dark shadow with a blurry face, a ghost. Now that he is ready, Antonio emerges from the bathroom dressed in black. He jumps out of the window before Leslie has a chance to see him. Like a ghost, he disappears into the night.

Dwight is seen coming out of the elevator. His pace was fast, and his expression was one of determination. He wasn't quite sure if he would be able to persuade Miss Davis to leave with him tonight. If the sun comes up and she starts to hemorrhage, there is no way that Dwight would be able to get Jimmy to the nearest hospital in time to save him. It is possible that Jimmy could lose his life. It is also possible that if Jimmy dies, Casandra may have a chance to live in Jimmy's body. It's very complicated to the point that it has Dwight's mind running around in circles. He rounds the corner. His breathing is heavy, and he has an eerie feeling in the pit of his stomach. Back at the nurse's station, Leslie is sitting in one of the empty chairs, sipping coffee and slowly rocking back and forth. She is calm and reflecting—thinking about her life's work. What she had done to a nine-year-old boy from a small town. She wanted to help him, but instead, she destroyed him and turned him into THE BLACK WIDOW'S GHOST.

"I didn't do anything to him that was worse than what he had already been through," she mused. "Oh, but see, that's where you're wrong," Dr. Ross turned around, and silhouetted by the hallway light was a dark figure holding a knife.

"What are you doing?"

"I am sorry, Mother, but I called the number you gave me. You were the first name on the list."

Dwight entered the hallway just in time to see Antonio's shadowed figure standing in the hall over Leslie's body and the chair. He had stabbed her. The knife was dripping and still soiled with her blood. Dwight guessed that he had stabbed her nine times—six in the chest and three in the neck. Before he could utter a word, Antonio had fled through an open window. Impressive, considering that the ward was on the third floor, Dwight thought to himself while chasing down the assailant. He ran to the window and cautiously looked outside—all around. There was no sign of The Black Widow's Ghost anywhere. Dwight quickly ran over to Leslie's lifeless body and checked for a pulse. He heard movement coming from down the hall and saw that the light in Casandra Davis' room was on. Dwight went to investigate. He pulled out his 35 mm high-point pistol and undid the safety. He crept towards the room. He approached the bed and could see that it was occupied."Dwight, it's me!" Lying in the bed was Casandra. She was in her hospital gown with the sash tied around her waist. She had a confused expression, and Dwight didn't know what to make of this surprise turn of events. He certainly did not know whether or not he was safe in her presence, knowing that somewhere inside of her was Antonio—fresh from a kill.

"Cassy?"

"Yes."

"Do you know where Antonio is?"

"I don't know where he is. Do you want me to try to find him? Is he in trouble?"

"Look, Sweetheart, he did some terrible things. People are going to start looking for him."

"Guess what? I found out tonight that Dr. Leslie is my real mother."

"Jimmy! Shut up!"

"N'... N'... NO wait. Is that little Jimmy? Little Jimmy! Can I talk to you?"

"Sorry, Dwight, it's past little Jimmy's bedtime."

"No, wait! Little Jimmy, where is Antonio?"

"He is in his room."

"Cassy, we have got to get you out of here! "Other Brother" is going to hunt you down next! Do you understand?"

"What is Other Brother?" Dwight realized that Casandra may have no clue that Other Brother even exists. If their paths have never crossed, and she knows very little about Antonio (at least that's what she tells everyone) or his dealings, she wouldn't be aware of Leslie and "Other Brother." Leslie would just be a therapist, and Dwight is just an "old flame." Antonio may not have shared his knowledge of Other Brother with her, either because the only contact Antonio had with Other Brother was through Leslie Ross. She could have treated him and had him trained, with Other Brother remaining a distant, anonymous, and silent partner.

"Grab your things. I know a place where we will be safe." Casandra put everything she had in a small duffle bag that was in the corner of the room. Dwight was able to sneak both of them out of the hospital undetected. Their only way out was down the same hallway that shared the lifeless body of Cassy's (former)therapist. Dwight is very cautious in case Cassy sees Leslie's body and decides to tell Antonio or Jimmy. She gasped at the pool of blood on the ground and the chair in the hallway. Dwight notices in passing that the chair is empty. The body of the deceased therapist was no longer there. Where did it go? Dwight quickly took a look around, but there was no trace of Dr. Leslie anywhere. Maybe she wasn't dead? Perhaps 'Other Brother' was there, conducting "damage control."

With no time to think, Dwight stayed focused on the escape route and getting Casandra out of the building and to the location that Dwight had in mind. They found the car. Moments later, they made it out of the parking lot.

"Where are you taking me?"

"Away from the hospital." Forty-five minutes later, they arrived at the old, familiar cabin that belonged to Kyle's family. Casandra got out of the vehicle and walked to the front door. She opened it up, and an overwhelming feeling of nostalgia came over her. Each picture and decoration was a reminder of a time gone by. "This is Kyle's dad's cabin."

"You've been here before?"

"Once. Kyle and I came here so that he could profess his undying love for me and throw his best friend under the bus."

"David?"

"Yes, He said that David didn't love me. That I was just a summer fling—a trick! Kyle said that he was the one who truly loved me and wanted to be with me forever. Of course, I went for David. David had more money and more confidence. Kyle was better-looking, but David was the total package."

"Cassy, you're a woman of a different sort. You are every man's dream. Kyle and David were sent to find you, but instead, they fell in love with you as I did."

"Right! You left me for married life, David is gone, and Kyle is missing. Every man's dream doesn't really hold much for me right now. Maybe I am just stressed out."

"I hear something outside. Stay here. I am going to have a look around." Casandra makes two cups of coffee and takes them outside on the front porch. She sits on the stairs and quietly waits for Dwight to come back to the cabin.

"Is that second cup of coffee for me?" Cassy looks up, and a large silhouette moves toward her. It was not Dwight.

"You better get out of here. Dwight is here with me. He'll be back any moment."

"What? You don't think I can take out the detective? I wrestled him and won back at the hospital. Remember that?" Kyle put one foot on the step and took Cassy's hand. Don't you think I have proven to you how much I care for you? It was I who brought you to the hospital the night David was killed. You would have bled out if I hadn't thrown you over my shoulder and brought you to your doctor. I could have taken you to National Jewish instead, but I knew that Leslie was your therapist and could help you heal." Kyle gets on his knees in front of her and leans in for a hug. Careful not to disturb the bandages underneath her hospital gown.

"We need to find you some clothes."

"Is it true that our meeting each other was planned? Leslie said that David and you were sent to capture me. I thought you loved me?"

"I love you. David wanted the bounty—the "finder's fee." I was willing to give up everything for you. I will run away with you right now if you want. Come on! Let's go!" He backs up and takes her hand. Her face changed. Her expression changed. Her voice was lower and more gruff. Kyle didn't know what was going on.

"She can't go with you right now." Antonio had come out of his room and was standing in front of Kyle, looking him right in the face. Kyle dropped the hand and realized that he was talking to the entity known as Antonio, "I know who you are. I read your file. You're the one they call 'The Black Widow's Ghost.'"

"I know who you are, too. You're Kyle Franco Templeman. Son and Heir to Franklin Jacob Templeman. The founder of Other Brother."

"Cassy doesn't know about Other Brother," Kyle said.

"Cassy doesn't know a lot of things."Antonio stood up and finished his coffee.

"Tell me, Antonio, how were you able to plunge the knife into David's body so deeply that it touched you with David on top of you? The physics doesn't add up."

"What makes you think that I took David's life? Jimmy took all of us away! He helped all of us escape from The Facility. We made it! I arrived in Chicago and met up with Zacklesbee, where we also met Casandra. She kept us hidden. After a while, we hoped that Other Brother would call off the search and we could have our lives back. Vidal told operatives that Kyle and David were sleeping with his star performer. So, the operatives put David on the list. The Mayor was already on the list, so all they had to do was add David. Frank sent Leslie to 'do the job.' She stole my spray and electronic signal to distort her appearance, took some Zeta Max, and David was history. She thought I was, too. But thanks to you, I survived. However, I was back in Leslie Ross' care—right where I started." Antonio chuckled at the irony of what she just said.

"I had no idea that you wanted out," Kyle said apologetically."I realize that now. Don't worry. You saved my life. I will spare you if you can get Cassy and all of us out of here and across the border to Canada so we can start a new life—free of Other Brother."

"I'll do it, but it won't be for you—I am doing this for Casandra. So, why are YOU here?"

"I was given one final list. There were only two names on the list. I took care of one. The other one is out there somewhere in the woods. So, stay out of sight until I complete this one last job. Then, Cassy is yours, and I will retreat to my room until we get to Canada." Kyle starts to back away, and Casandra comes back. Kyle slips away into the shadows of the trees. Casandra sits on the front porch. An out-of-breath Dwight Hussleman comes bounding up to the front of the cabin. Casandra is waiting for him. He is looking at her, but something isn't right. He ignores it and looks at the coffee cups. They are both empty. "Did you drink both of those?"

"I was cold." Well, let's go inside and get you warm," Dwight says. They enter the cabin, and Dwight makes them a fresh pot. The rain is coming down steadily now, and flashes of lightning begin to light up the night sky.

Sharon and Jerry Mack are shuffling papers back at headquarters. "I still question why Dwight is taking such an interest in this case. I thought he was looking for another feather in his cap. That's not it. I thought he wanted to take down the organization known as Other Brother. Now I realize that it's because of the girl, Casandra, or Jimmy. What do you think?" Jerry Mack mused while shuffling papers.

"He's a good detective. He doesn't always disclose his motives, but his hunches are almost always spot on. We would do well to follow his lead, sir." Sharon returned.

"Yes, but as a male, when a female is involved..."

"Well, Jimmy is not a female."

"Sharon, in my experience, as a police officer and detective and now the Commissioner, I have seen a lot. Gender is tricky, and it serves to protect and expose the best in us and the worst in us. Beauty has no gender. Charm can be expressed by either sex. One is only deceived by the appearance of a transformed individual if one wants to be. The seduction, the appearance, all five senses are engaged when face to face with Trans people."

"You think Dwight is compromised? That he is incapable of staying objective."

"Remember. It was Beauty that killed 'The Beast.'" Jerry Mack looked Sharon eye to eye and turned towards the door. "Do you want another cup?"

"Sure. Thanks, Jerry." Sharon looked back at Jerry Mack and flashed him a smile. She paused for a moment and realized that if Dwight is not thinking clearly—as Jerry Mack is suggesting, then Dwight needs her more than anything right now. He needs someone there, able to handle the situation if he is compromised. She grabbed her coat and headed out into the storm. Her first destination is Mercy Hospital, where Dwight is with Cassy and carrying out his plan to bait Antonio into exposing himself. He has several doses of manufactured Zeta Max. The effects of such a powerful drug could have catastrophic complications and could put her partner in jeopardy. One more turn and she enters the parking lot at the North Entrance. She arrives on the third floor. It is eerily quiet. There was one room in the ward that had a light on—that must be Cassy's room, but she couldn't hear any noise and didn't see any shadows moving in the background. There were no nurses and no other patients on this floor. At 3 am, the office was clean and organized. The floor was freshly mopped. It was almost too clean. She pulled out her 35mm Glock and held it at the ready. She slowly eased into the doorway and peeked around the corner. The room was empty. Upon further investigation, Sharon found traces of blood smeared on the floor and wall in the corner closet. Dwight and Cassy were nowhere to be seen. She wanders over to the bed, and there are no clues left on the mattress or the sheets. The heart monitor's last reading was "normal."

"Where are you, buddy?" She wondered out loud as if to utter a request to the universe to find her partner. She called for backup to the hospital and requested that they bring the supplies to conduct a blood test on the floor and the wall. Jerry Mack responded that he was on his way personally. He was now invested and wanted to see for himself the outcome. Sharon continued to the bathroom. There was a small plastic cup by the sink used to dispense pharmaceuticals. There was dark liquid in the toilet that smelled like turpentine. In the corner were a Lego and a toy soldier. If Dwight were in love with Casandra and knew that Other Brother would come looking for her, he would want to take her away somewhere safe and protect her. That would mean harboring a cold-blooded killer that is locked inside of her as well. The most secluded place would have to be in the rural countryside just outside the city. She bolted out of the hospital and sped away to the only place she knew that would be familiar to Casandra and Dwight—Kyle's Cabin. She called in to update Jerry Mack on her whereabouts. Jerry had just arrived at the hospital and started the investigation by having the whole third floor quarantined as a crime scene. He called an APB on Dr Leslie to try to locate her body.

"Careful, Kyle was spotted on the Highway at a convenience store filling up with gas. He may be on his way to where you're heading. He is driving a white sedan with Illinois plates RFK 676."

"I will definitely keep an eye out."

"I am sending a detachment to the cabin. It should reach you there within the hour. Don't do anything brave until officers arrive. Do you understand? DO NOT ENGAGE THE SUSPECT!"

"Roger that!" Sharon drove on. Her breathing was beginning to accelerate. She was unprepared for this. They don't teach you this kind of thing at the academy. Things you learn there are usually cut and dry, but who knows what awaits her at the cabin. She came to the road that leads to the cabin and parked the car at a safe distance from the front walkway. With her pistol in readiness, she quietly tries to make her way undetected to the front steps of the cabin. She would have gotten to the front door when the ringer on her phone started to sound. Sharon had forgotten to silence her phone on the approach, and the noise was close enough to be heard by the occupants of the lodge. She silenced it within seconds and regained her composure. She was mentally "beating herself up," wondering how she could have been so stupid. She walked back towards her vehicle and saw that the call came from Jerry Mack back at the hospital. It went to voicemail.

"Sharon! It's Jerry. I hope this message reaches you before it is too late. The cybersecurity lab just called me to let me know that there was activity on the Other Brother Website. You're not going to like this. A new list was issued, and there were only two names on it. Leslie was one of those names. We have reason to believe that she has already been murdered, although we haven't been able to locate the body. You'll never believe who the second name on the list is...it's Dwight! Sharon, you've got to find Dwight before Antonio tries to kill him. Proceed with extreme caution. I repeat. Dwight is the target—use extreme caution!"

Sharon heightened her awareness of the surroundings. The only things she had to guide her steps were her cell phone and the light of the moon. She could hear that something was following her. It was behind her and to the right. Too big to be a creature. A bear? A cougar? There was a lone street light just outside the perimeter, and the cabin lights illuminated her path. She headed toward the cabin, anxious to rescue her partner. She was his only chance at survival.

# Chapter Fifteen-Love is a Two-Edged Sword

Sharon was "fueled." Her adrenaline was pumping as hard as the heart in her chest. She understood why veterans of the force were heavily medicated and socially lubricated. Each case presents a series of challenges that can render even the toughest of the toughest damages beyond any justice that has been served. She fears that it will be her fate as well. Slowly creeping toward the edge of the property, Sharon feels that the person or persons following her are still there and catching up to her. It doesn't matter. She is almost there. The door opens, and she sees a man carrying a five-gallon can. It is red in color, which typically indicates that it contains some type of fuel, such as gasoline. He sets it outside the door, and the bright flickering orange of a fire can be seen through the split in the curtains. She spies another figure moving about. It is not as tall. It is not as large as the man who stepped outside. The man must be Dwight. Her guess is that the other figure inside the cabin is Casandra/Jimmy/ Antonio. Little Jimmy is there, too.

"What happens, Dwight, when night turns and the sun starts to rise in the east?" Casandra is taken by the warmth of the fire and the presence of her handsome protector. Dwight was also impassioned by the warm glow on Casandra's beautiful face, a face that he had longed to hold in his hands for the rest of his life. His thoughts of her were not the same as when they first met. She is not the same person. He couldn't escape the fact that she was also Antonio, a cold, blood-thirsty, trained assassin. He just stared. Dwight contemplated what he would have to do to lure Antonio out in the open, out of 'his room.'

"I've saved up some money. Let's go! Let's get out of here and go somewhere quiet, where no one will find us. It can be just you and me."

Dwight understood the dangerous game he was playing. He knew that he was dancing too close to the fire. It was a one-way ticket on a train bound for nowhere. He's afraid that there is a tunnel up ahead, and he won't be able to see his way out.

"But you didn't answer my question. You know that Jimmy will not be able to survive the rising of the sun, don't you? What happens when Jimmy wakes up? When the sun comes up, what then?" Cassy was frightened. She feared for her survival, real or imagined. Dwight moved closer toward her.

"Cassy, you know that Jimmy is all in your mind, right?"

"Jimmy is a part of me. He is the root! It is not possible to live without him! Why can't you see that? I wasn't there when he was born.  I was created by him to hide all of us.  If it weren't for Jimmy Rantor, I would not be here, and if he dies, I think I would die with him." Cassy didn't like his tone and his dismissive demeanor.

"How do you know? Have you seen what would happen if you tried to separate from the rest of them and just stood alone, by yourself?" Dwight takes Cassy's hands and helps her stand on her feet. You are a part of you, and you are fine. There is no damage to your body, no bruising, no bleeding. Look!" Dwight removes the hospital gown, "but we have to find you some clothes." The scars were gone. They weren't pronounced but noticeable. However, Cassy couldn't see them anywhere.

"That's funny, Kyle said the same..." Cassy remembered that Kyle was waiting for her outside. She turned and felt a presence in her ear, "Don't even think about it, Cassy." Dwight noticed that Cassy's expression had changed.

"What is it?"

"He is here." She said in a terrified whisper. "He is right behind me. He wants me to take the pill."

"What happens when you take the pill?"

"He becomes a weapon." Cassy becomes agitated and nervous. She starts to quiver. Dwight covers her with a blanket. She is still shaking, "He says that if I don't take the pill. He will kill little Jimmy. Dwight, I don't know what to do. Dwight, what do I do? Don't let me die!" Dwight didn't answer. He was all out of answers. He is not equipped with the tools or the training to handle Dissociative Identity Disorder. This was beyond his realm of expertise. It was a cry for help; he didn't know how to answer. Dwight realized that he was looking at his love and hate personified face to face, and he was gobsmacked. Actually, she was broken into four parts. To destroy any of them was to destroy a part of her. Life forced her to create these entities to protect her body and mind. Only, they were twisted by the influences of Dr. Leslie and 'Other Brother.' To kill one could risk damaging them all. The best solution is to integrate all of them together slowly, but there was no time. Antonio was created to protect the others. If Antonio is taken out of the equation, Cassy and the others could be left constantly vulnerable, in a perpetual state of fear. He gave them courage, confidence, and a sense of security. Little Jimmy is the child who was left behind. He represents the innocence that was robbed from him at an early age. The people, chosen by the Gods to care for Jimmy, love him and protect him, abandoned Little Jimmy and left him to wander, scared and alone. They exploited and abused him in the most cruel and detestable manner. No one came. He called out, but no one came, searching for love in the dark and cold world. He will remain forever nine years old. Jimmy is the root. After enduring the relentless abuse from everyone in his life, being trained in and out of "The Facility" of Other Brother, and an attempt on his life, his body can't take much more. His soul was so broken, and his mind was so twisted, that he developed the power to solve his dilemma. Jimmy embodies that human spirit in all of us that thinks of new and creative ways to survive the worst that this life dishes out. Yet, he is so brutalized that when the sun comes up, he dies a little more every day. That is why they all need each other. They are all Jimmy's family. Dwight began to feel the conflict well up inside him.

He looks at Casandra with love and longing, passion and despair. His arms tightened around her waist, and she sighed and gazed into his eyes. He was strong. She felt delicate in his arms. She was beginning to realize what she needed to do.

"I can't do it. I can't go with you. I couldn't then before I married Misty, and I can't now. I thought I could, but I can't," he crumbles to his knees. Miss Davis had brought him down. Dwight considered himself to be masculine and indestructible, but he was no match for the Black Widow's Ghost. He was too overwhelmed. It was too much for his masculinity to process. He did not have the tools to undo the damage that this goddess had done to him. "Step aside, sister." Dwight looked up, and there she stood, but it wasn't her. She had a scowl on her face. Her eyes were looking right through him. She saw a lost pile of betrayal, wrapped up in guilt, with linebacker shoulders and a chiseled jawline, lying on the edge of a pier in the rain. "This is going to be a piece of cake," Antonio announced. Then he flew across the room as if someone had thrown him. He slammed against a wall , knocking down pictures and busting a table lamp. The light bulb had busted, and little shards of glass were all over the floor.

Dwight was dumbfounded. He had no idea why that happened. He realized that there was an inner conflict going on inside Jimmy as well. Dwight couldn't believe what was unfolding right before his eyes. Jimmy lies there for a minute. Dwight stands up and goes over to see if they are okay. Casandra rose from the floor, brushed off some of the loose glass, and looked at Dwight. Dwight went into panic mode and prepared for anything to happen. His senses were engaged while staring straight at his possible demise. He raised his hands and made fists just in case the person he was looking at was someone he didn't want to see.

It's me!" Casandra held up two hands and slowly moved away from the wall and towards Dwight.

"A moment ago, I was staring someone in the face."

"That was Antonio, not me."

"Where's Antonio now?"

"I locked him away in his room." She slowed her pace, but Dwight still wasn't letting his guard down. "What if Antonio breaks the door down? What happens then?"

"He won't break it down."

"How are you able to do that? Lock him away like that?"

"The same way I am going to attempt to heal Jimmy before the sun comes up."

"I'm sorry, this is a little confusing to me. I thought I could handle it, but I'm not sure."

"We have to think of something soon; the sun will rise, and then I won't be able to go anywhere."

"Okay, if the sun comes up and Jimmy can't recover, or we can't get him to a hospital in time, you may have to let him go."

"You mean let him die? You want me to abandon Jimmy like everyone he's ever met in his life? No, I will find a way to heal him before I let him die!"

"Okay, I have no doubt that you can do it. While you are doing that, I will start loading up the car so we can get the hell out of here." Dwight started packing things in a bag. He walked outside, and standing in the illumination of the lone street light in the yard was Kyle. The day was over, and the sun was starting to descend. The cooler temperature raised a choir of insects and bird calls. Dwight set his bags slowly on the ground and walked to where Kyle was standing. "You still believe I killed my best friend?"

"I know that he was on 'Other Brother's Hit List. Since you don't work for 'Other Brother,' I figured it wasn't you."

"It was Leslie who plunged the knife into my friend," Kyle starts crying, "My buddy..."

"How did you know that Cassy was here, Kyle?"

"This cabin has been in my family for three generations. We chose this location because of its beauty and privacy. I just assumed it's the reason why you chose it too, to hide Casandra, to hide Antonio."

"Well, we were just leaving."

"I hope that you don't believe that she is going with you."

"I'm not going to just abandon her and Jimmy. Don't you think that she has had enough and deserves a life of peace, companionship, and prosperity in a place where no one knows her?"

"She's coming with me. I'm taking her to Canada. We can start a new life there."

"What about Other Brother?" Kyle tackled Dwight and took him to the ground in a typical Greco-Roman style. This time, Dwight was ready for him. He punches Kyle in the nose. Kyle returns with a punch to the gut. Dwight, in keeping with the boxing strategy, delivered an uppercut to Kyle's jaw. Kyle was not phased by the jaw punch. Dwight busted his hand, and it was bleeding. Kyle grabs Dwight by the waist and shifts his weight off balance to do a hip toss to the ground. He lands on top of Dwight and rolls onto his back. To try to put Dwight in a chokehold. He grabbed Kyle's arm to try to loosen his grip.

"You're on the list! Do you hear me? You're on the list!" Dwight surrendered to the hold, and Kyle loosened his grip. The two cautiously got off the ground and stood face to face.

"I came to get Antonio and take them across the border to Canada."

"You never answered my question. What about Other Brother?"

"You probably know that my father is Dean Frank Templeman, Leslie's mentor, and is deeply involved with Other Brother."

"We have all of the intel on you and your father, Kyle."

"That's probably why they put you on Antonio's Hit List. You are a loose end and need to be taken out."

"What do you mean I am on the list?"

"When Leslie gave Antonio his final hit list, there were only two names listed on it. I don't know who the first one was, but you were the second. Antonio told me himself."

"The first was Leslie Ross, Jimmy's psychiatrist. Put your hands in the air, Kyle." He complies.

"You are under arrest for conspiring to transport a known suspect across the border. That also makes you an accomplice to murder in the first degree for the death of Mayor Kinsingsworth and his son, David. Kinsingsworth," Sharon stated as she approached the scene, wielding her weapon, "Get on the ground."

"Wait, Sharon, don't do this!"

"Dwight, I will be happy to talk with you after I put the cuffs on Kyle." Dwight took the gun out of Sharon's hand, and Kyle hit her in the head and knocked her out. The blow rendered her unconscious. Dwight ran into the house. "Is she dead?"

"Stick around, you'll find out..."

"We have to get Cassy out of here."

"I know you're not leaving without me."

"Fine, you get her in the car, and I will grab our things.

"ANTONIO!" said a loud voice coming from a bullhorn. It was Jerry Mack. The Chicago police force was deployed around the cabin. They were moving into position. "We have the area surrounded! Come out with your hands up!" Sharon was rolling around on the ground. Once her vision cleared, she was able to see that Jerry Mack had arrived. Dwight and Kyle were both still in the yard, just a few feet ahead of her position. She was close to apprehending the suspect, Antonio. If she can get past the two men and get inside the cabin, she has a good shot at arresting the Black Widow's Ghost—the first feather in her cap. A shot was heard. It came from inside the cabin. Dwight and Kyle look at each other. "Cassy must have found Daddy's hunting rifle." Kyle followed Dwight inside. "Don't you mean Antonio?"

"Whoever." Another shot was fired that started a gun battle between Antonio and the Chicago Police Department. Dwight and Kyle were caught in the crossfire. So, when they got to the front porch, bullets were already flying. Sounds of splitting timber and shattering glass could be heard for miles. Screams from officers who had been hit were heard from every direction. Others, hit by shrapnel, fell to the ground in pain. Kyle ran off into the woods, and Dwight ran into the cabin. The police entered the house through the front door. The smell of gas was strong in the living room and the bedrooms. Sharon noticed that the gas can on the front porch was no longer there. Officers continued to search the house. It was cleared. No trace was found of Cassy, Kyle, or Dwight. "The house is clear!"

Sharon was already headed to the back porch as Dwight and Kyle were leaving the cabin. "Where is Antonio? I can't let you take him!"

"Sharon, she is not Antonio!"

"She killed Lillie!" Her outburst was an indicator that Sharon's feelings of revenge were clouding her judgment. She took a breath and regained her composure. However, no amount of composure could hide her disappointment in Dwight. She looked up to him, a respected member of the force and mentor, who betrayed her trust and integrity for a murderer for hire.

"Come on, Dwight! You know it's not true. She is Antonio. She is a Murderer."

"Sharon, I can't...I can't let you take her. She needs me! I'll take care of her!"

"Dwight, move out of the way! I am taking her into custody!"

"SHARON!..." Dwight lunged for her pistol, but she fired it. Kyle was in the trees waiting for the smoke to clear when he heard the shotgun fire again. It was another rifle shot, so he doubled back to see if Casandra was okay. The sun was peeking out over the horizon, and Cassy was changing. She turned pale, and blood started to leak from her abdomen. They needed to make their escape. Kyle returned to the cabin and saw Dwight and Sharon both lying on the ground. Standing behind Sharon was Cassy, dressed in a hospital gown with a piece of fabric tied around her waist. She held the same shotgun that she had found inside the cabin. It was smoking. She was weak, and Kyle sprang into action. Dwight grabbed Sharon's hand, and Sharon accidentally squeezed the trigger. Dwight fell to the ground. At the same time, Cassy aimed at Sharon and shot her. She fell on top of Dwight. Too weak to make it off the porch, Kyle snatched her up and carried them down the hill to the car. "Cassy, stay with me."

"We have to go NOW! Jimmy is going to die, Kyle! And there is nothing I can do to help him. They got 50 paces away from the cabin and...BOOM! The cabin blew up! Flames shot out of the doors and the roof. A second explosion blew the roof into a million pieces. The windows burst, sending shards of glass flying into the air. The sound sent Kyle and Cassy to the ground. Kyle went back to help Cassy get to her feet. She was fading fast, so Kyle hoisted her onto his shoulders and carried her down the hill to the car that was waiting there. He secured her to the passenger seat and hopped in the driver's seat. Down the road, they went. In the rearview mirror, he could see the fire trucks pulling up to the scene. With a step on the gas pedal, they were off. Down the road, they drove until they got to the Canadian border.

"Change of plans, Kyle."

"What about Jimmy?"

"He's gone now." Kyle noticed her sinister tone. Was he addressing Antonio? How did Antonio escape "his room?" He decided to put his questions away. He was just thankful to escape all the chaos. Was it just Jimmy who died? And what effect will Jimmy's passing have on his body, especially at nighttime? They will likely find out as they approach their destination.

"Where are we going, Miss Davis, my love?"

"New York, Baby...New York!" Kyle turns around. Cassy is passed out. He changes route for the Big Apple.

"Good Job, I'll be in my room if you need me." Staring at the open road, Kyle wasn't sure who uttered that ominous phrase. He can almost picture the door of a room closing, and Antonio turning around to say: "Bye, for now. The dawn is breaking, and the clouds on the horizon are clear. But every time you see a FLASH and a CLAP! Remember me, The Black Widow's Ghost, and know that I am near. "STAY OFF THE LIST!"

The End.

# About the Author

J.K. Rennaker is a debut novelist and storyteller based in Springfield, Missouri. As a multicultural and non-binary creator, Rennaker brings a unique and inclusive voice to fiction, blending emotional depth with high-stakes storytelling.

Their work explores identity, survival, and transformation — often reflecting the complexity of their own lived experiences growing up in a rural town as a person of color and part of the LGBTQ+ community.

Black Widow's Ghost is the first novel in a planned trilogy and marks the beginning of a bold new voice in psychological thriller fiction.

www.ingramcontent.com/pod-product-compliance
Lightning Source LLC
Chambersburg PA
CBHW020802310726

48969CB00002B/664